THE COLLAPSE OF ORDINARY

Steve L Clark

Orange Octave Press

PRAISE FOR THE COLLAPSE OF ORDINARY

"Each story boldly pushes the limits, stretching darkness over your mind like a cloak. Haunting visions still plague me long afterwards. Steve L Clark is a superstar." – Chuck Buda, author of Boondock Butcher

"A masterful execution of horror and suspense. Steve L Clark is an up and coming horror writer that deserves your attention." – Matt Wildasin, author of Melancholia

WORKS BY STEVE L CLARK

Novellas

The Doors of Chamberlain

Down Home

Short Story Collections

The Collapse of Ordinary

Twisting Parallels

For Dad and my brother Donald.

When we see each other again, I'll tell you all about it.

CONTENTS

INTRODUCTION

They're coming to get you, Barbara!

That line was the beginning of a lifelong fascination with horror. Thanks to a horror loving older brother, I saw that zombie knock Johnny down and smash his head on a gravestone at the age of five or six. I never looked back. I grew up on a steady diet of horror movies (some of which I was probably too young to be watching), horror books, and comics. What started with *Goosebumps* led to *Fear Street* and then Stephen King. My brother had a few EC Comics reprints, introducing me to *Tales From the Crypt, The Vault of Horror,* and *The Haunt of Fear.* I loved the short story format and the twist endings that often closed out those stories. I imagine that influence will be noticeable within these pages.

Fast forward through a couple decades of entertaining the idea of being a writer but never actually writing anything. I started listening to podcasts and came across *The Horror Show with Brian Keene.* Something that really piqued my interest was co-host Matt Wildasin had just released his debut short story collection *Edge of Twilight.* I picked up the book and really enjoyed it. As I listened to discussions on the podcast about the beginning stages of his writing career, I was inspired. I realized this is what I wanted to do. I reached out to Matt on a whim to chat about his process and experiences starting out, and he graciously agreed.

He was kind enough to read a couple of early stories and give advice. From there, I was off and running.

It wasn't always easy. In fact, it was almost never easy. There were a lot of droughts; weeks at a time when I wouldn't write a single word. I kept at it, and eventually the stories formed. Some of them came to me in a flash, and the story was written in a day or two (Those That Help Themselves). Other stories took a long time and a rewrite or two before they ended up where they are today (Easter Morning).

Ultimately, I am proud of each story in this book. They all mean something to me. I hope they will mean something to you as well. Maybe these stories creep you out. Some of them might make you laugh. Others might make you uncomfortable. If I've done this right, you will feel something.

Welcome to The Collapse of Ordinary.

THE NIGHT AUDITOR

K eith Hellickson leaned back in his chair, dropped his head back to see the tall peak of the A-frame roof, and exhaled deeply.

I'm so fucking bored.

He thought about how much he'd rather crash out on his couch at home. His eyelids drooped heavily. Realizing how close he was to falling asleep, he quickly jerked himself upright and scanned the lobby.

That's all I need, he thought. *A guest complaining to Mr. Creighton about the guy at the front desk sleeping on the job.*

Keith was two weeks into his new position as the night auditor of the Terra Bay Resort. The job comprised filing the sales receipts for the hotel dining room and managing the front desk during the overnight hours. From 10:00 pm to 5:00 am, Keith and the night shift maintenance man, Hank Allen, were the only working staff at the resort. Hank stayed downstairs in the maintenance room most of the time. Only once, when a guest's heater had gone on the fritz, had Keith radioed Hank for help. Hank was friendly enough to talk to, but he didn't volunteer himself to conversation often. So, for most of his shift, Keith was alone.

Alone and fucking bored.

The paperwork portion of his work only took up an hour or two, depending on how busy the dining room had been. Aside from any late arrivals he might have to check in, there was very little to do after midnight other than be available if a guest needed anything.

On this night, only seven of the hotel's seventy-two rooms were occupied. The chances of a guest needing anything were slim to none.

With a sigh, Keith rose from his chair and stretched. He wore the standard Terra Bay uniform; khakis and a maroon polo shirt with a gold name tag pinned to the chest. He ran a hand over his buzzed head while stifling another yawn and walked casually around the counter and into the lobby. He stopped just short of the sensor that would open the sliding glass doors and looked out into the parking lot. Light poles illuminated small areas, but the thick foliage of the woods pressed in toward the building, creating a wall of darkness beyond. The forest was beautiful in the daytime, especially in the fall, when the leaves turned various shades of red and orange. At night, it took on a more sinister appearance, dark and foreboding.

Shaking his head at himself, Keith wandered across the lobby and peered down the east hall. Red and yellow lights from the game room arcades flashed sporadically on the walls. Beyond that, he saw the empty hallway of the east wing of guest rooms. A large spiral staircase domi-nated the middle of the lobby. Down those stairs were the dining room, lounge, and west wing of guest rooms.

A loud chirp rang out behind him and he spun around. Wide eyed, he searched the lobby for the source of the noise but saw nothing. After a tense few seconds, just as he allowed himself to relax a bit, the noise rang out again, this time followed by a burst of static and a voice.

"Hey Keith, you copy?" the voice asked.

"Jesus Christ," he said, realization dawning on him. Feeling foolish, he hurried back around the counter and snatched up the radio from the desk.

"Hank, you scared the shit out of me," Keith said into the two-way radio.

"Sorry 'bout that, boss," Hank said with a chuckle. "Just wanted to let you know I'll be outside for a bit. Creighton asked me to check out a problem with the pool filter. I'll have the radio if you need me."

"All right," Keith replied. He paused and then hit the button on the radio again. "Hey Hank, what do you do all night to entertain yourself? You know, when you're not fixing pool filters."

Keith stared at the radio, waiting for a reply. They had never really had any conversations not strictly work related, and Keith wasn't sure how Hank would take the random question.

"You bored already?" Hank asked.

Keith could hear the humor in Hank's voice and relaxed.

"Yeah, you could definitely say that," Keith replied.

"You read? Read a book. That's what I do."

Keith frowned. He hadn't read a book willingly since elementary school. Being forced to read literary classics in high school had done a number on his interest in books.

"Nah, not a reader," Keith answered.

"Of course not," Hank said with a hint of sarcasm in his tone. "You millennials are all the same. If it ain't on Netflix or a smartphone, you don't want nothing to do with it."

"You sound like a grumpy old man," Keith said.

"Uh huh. How about you listen to a podcast then? I'm not so old that I don't know what they are. It's like reading, but without the work."

That's not a bad idea, he thought.

"You got any suggestions?" Keith asked.

Nearly twenty seconds passed with no reply from Hank. Keith's brow furrowed as he considered the delayed response. He was just about to ask again when the radio crackled to life.

"Do you like scary stories?" Hank asked. "There's a podcast I listen to from time to time. It's called Terror Beyond Reason. Voice actors tell you a story. Like listening to an old radio broadcast."

Keith considered. As bored as he was, the thought of listening to ghost stories while he sat alone inside a nearly empty hotel in the middle of a forest made him feel uneasy.

"I don't know Hank," he answered. "Not sure if I'm in the mood for ghost stories."

"Yeah, I figured as much,"

Keith looked incredulously at the radio. *Is he taunting me right now?*

"What's that supposed to mean?" Keith asked, a hard edge in his voice.

"Now don't get your panties in a bunch," Hank said, laughing. "I didn't mean to offend you. Some folks just don't like to be scared. I get it."

Keith felt his face flush. He didn't know why he gave a rat's ass what the old maintenance man thought, but he did. Some underlying part of him was ashamed of himself. *This old guy thinks I'm a pussy.*

"Don't sweat it, boss," Hank said. "I got to get moving or I'll have to explain to Creighton that the pool filter is still broken because I spent all night jacking my jaws with you. Call me if you have any troubles."

"All right, will do."

He sat the radio back down on the desk and dropped into his chair. His phone was sitting next to the computer mouse on the desk, and he swiped it up. After a few minutes of scrolling through social media, he sighed and opened the podcast app. He tapped the magnifying glass icon and typed Terror Beyond Reason into the search field.

In an instant, he decided he would listen to Hank's scary story podcast, and he would tell Hank all about how it didn't scare him. Normally, Keith prided himself on his lack of concern over what other people thought about him. Here, he couldn't shake the feeling he had disappointed Hank with his refusal to listen to a horror story.

I'll show him. Hell, I might even like it.

After a few seconds, the podcast app search finished and produced a No Matches Found notice. Keith frowned.

He debated giving up. He wanted to show Hank he wasn't scared, but he also didn't feel like downloading any new software to play an obscure horror podcast he normally would have no interest in. Reluctantly, he opened the phone's web browser and typed Terror Beyond Reason into the search field.

A list of websites appeared, but the first several findings did not appear to be podcast related. There were a few amateur blogs, a website for a band pushing horror-themed punk music, and several random pages featuring the words "terror", "beyond", and "reason" somewhere in the keywords.

With resignation, Keith swiped up on his phone to close out the search window. As he did so, the page scrolled up a bit more and the next result caught his attention. The link title read, "This is the terror you are looking for!" Keith frowned. Aside from the title, there was no description of the website listed.

Are you the terror I'm looking for? Keith asked himself. After a brief debate, he tapped the link. The page loaded instantly to reveal a solid black background with a single red hyperlink in the middle of the page that simply read BEGIN.

Keith stared at his phone. Surely, this wasn't the podcast Hank was talking about. There were no episodes listed, no credit information, no information of any kind. Just that single red link.

Keith considered a moment. His eyes dragged across the digital clock on the desk. 12:17am. Nearly five hours to go in his shift. With the weight of boredom pressing in, he tapped the link. *This better not be malware,* he thought.

Immediately, the link was replaced with an audio file and his phone speaker came to life. He pressed the volume up button a couple times and the sound of trees rustling in a strong wind became apparent. A rhythmic crunch suggested someone walking through mounds of fallen leaves. After a moment, a man spoke.

"At last, you have arrived. Faced with fear, you have declared that you are not afraid. You will listen to our tale of terror. You will not shy away from the dark. Bold and brave you must be! Though I wonder what will become of you when our story ends. When you have seen what awaits you on the other side, in the dark. Will you remain unchanged? I wonder. I wonder very much. Let us delay no further. Brace yourself, my friend, as we visit 'The Hotel!'"

Keith rolled his eyes and cocked his head to the side. *Of course, it would be a hotel story. Why wouldn't it be?*

A thunderclap erupted from the speaker of his phone, causing Keith to flinch in his chair. He felt his face flush and was relieved that no one else was around to see his reaction.

"We begin our tale at the front desk where the young man at the counter is about to find out that one of his guests is not quite who they seem to be," the narrator continued.

The voice fell silent, and Keith stared at his phone as he waited out the dramatic pause. Seconds passed and turned into a half minute before he grabbed his phone to see if the file had stopped. The audio player continued to tick off the seconds. He tapped the speaker icon to be sure the player hadn't somehow been muted, but the volume bar was nearly at full.

"Oh, come on," he mumbled to himself. He tried pausing and then playing the file again, to no success. The file played on in silence.

Annoyed, Keith tapped the window button to close out the website. When the window did not shrink, he tapped the button again. Nothing. He grabbed the tail of his polo shirt, rubbed the screen of his phone clean, and tapped again. Nothing.

What the hell?

A thought dawned on him, and he let out an aggravated groan. *A virus. I fucking knew it!*

As a last-ditch effort, he held down the power button to reset the phone. The old "turn it off and back on" trick usually fixed most problems. Once again, the phone did not respond. The audio file continued to play on in silence, but beyond that, it had rendered his phone useless.

"You've got to be kidding me," he said.

"Is this a bad time?" asked a woman's voice.

Keith snapped to attention to find a young woman standing a few feet from the desk. She wore gray sweatpants and a baggy t-shirt. Her brown hair was pulled up into a messy bun and, judging by the state of her eyes, she had recently been asleep.

"I'm sorry, ma'am, I didn't see you come in. How can I help you?" Keith asked as he got to his feet. He could feel himself blushing from embarrassment. How long had she been standing there watching him play with his phone? How the hell did she get all the way through the lobby without him noticing?

"What time does the dining room open for breakfast?" she asked. "I don't sleep well, so I went for a walk around the hotel. I saw you here and thought I would ask."

"Of course, ma'am. The dining room opens at 6:00 am," he replied.

"Ok, thank you," the woman said. She turned and started back across the lobby toward the flashing lights of the game room.

"If there's anything else I can do for you, please call or stop by the desk," Keith called out after her.

The woman turned and gave him a polite smile and nodded before continuing.

Keith heard the soft whoosh of the double doors closing as she entered the east wing corridor. Swiftly, he moved around the counter and crossed the lobby to peer after her. He caught only a glimpse before she reached the branch in the hall and was out of sight. Frowning, he returned to the desk. *Where did she come from?* If she came from the east wing, he would've heard the doors open. The main entrance sliding doors would've made even more noise. It was possible she could've come up the stairs from the west wing, but he felt like he would've seen her passing across the lobby rather than being surprised by her right in front of him.

Guess I really zoned out, he thought as he dropped back into his chair. He reached to pick up his cell phone, but just before his fingers touched the glass, the front desk phone jingled to life.

Keith looked at the clock on the desk to see it was now going on one o'clock in the morning. A front desk call at this time of night was probably not a good thing. Bracing himself for the potential problems, he picked up the phone.

"Front desk, this is Keith speaking. How can I help you?"

"Uh yeah, hi," said a gravelly male voice. "I think there's a party or something going on down the hall, and I'm hearing squealing and laughing in the hallway. Thought I heard a scream. Woke me up."

"Oh, I see," Keith replied. "Can you tell me your room number, sir?"

"Uh, yeah. Hold on a minute," the man said.

Keith heard the knock of the nightstand as the man put the phone down, and then the faint squeak of bedsprings. After a few seconds, the receiver scraped against the table again.

"It's room 62," the man replied. "Christ, sounds like it's right outside in the hallway."

"Okay, sir. Thank you for reporting this, and I apologize for the inconvenience. I will see to it myself and ask them to call it a night. Please call me back if you have any more problems."

"Okay. Thank you," the man answered.

Keith hung up the phone and stood. It wasn't unusual for a group to get a little rowdy from time to time. The lounge was a full-service bar. It closed at 10 pm, but that didn't stop people from continuing the party in their rooms. The other possibility was kids. Sometimes you would have a family staying with children that weren't being supervised as well as they should have been.

Normally, Keith would radio Hank to check out the complaint, and then he would call the room if necessary. Leaving the front desk un-manned was not ideal. In this situation, he had no choice. With Hank outside working on the pool, it would take too much time to get him inside to investigate. By then, the man in room 62 would probably have called back. It was fair to assume a second call for the same issue would not be as friendly.

Keith grabbed the radio in case Hank needed to reach him and crossed the lobby. Rooms 37 through 72 were down the east wing, so he hurried through the game room and through the double doors.

Silence welcomed him in the hall as he entered. He walked silently; the carpet absorbed the sound of his hurried steps. He listened intently for any noise coming from a guest room, but heard nothing. He slowed as he came to the branch in the hallway. Cautiously, he peaked around the corner, hoping to find the culprits in action. The hall was empty.

Keith walked the rest of the hall, glancing at room 62 as he passed. He stopped at the far end, the dim red glow of the emergency EXIT sign shining on his face. Standing motionless, he strained his ears. He heard nothing. No televisions, no conversations, no showers running. Nothing.

Moving back up the hallway, he hesitated outside of room 62 and considered knocking to notify the man that whoever he had been hearing seemed to have packed it in for the night.

Better not, he thought. If the man had gone back to sleep, he probably wouldn't be thrilled to be woken again just to be told he could sleep now.

Satisfied with his decision, Keith closed the distance to the double doors and emerged back into the game room. He took two strides before abruptly coming to a halt.

The girl from the front desk stood in the middle of the game room, her glassy-eyed stare fixed on him.

"Shit!" he exclaimed. "I beg your pardon, ma'am. You scared me."

The girl stared back blankly at him. The arcade lights flashed hypnotically off her face. Dizziness gripped him the longer she held his gaze.

At last, she blinked, and her expression softened. "That's okay," she said. "I shouldn't be sneaking up on people in the middle of the night."

"It's fine, really," he said. "Say, have you seen or heard any other guests the last few minutes? I had a noise complaint, but I didn't hear anything when I checked?"

"No, I haven't," she answered. "They're all quiet for now."

Keith looked at her quizzically.

"I should get to bed," she said.

"Okay. Thank you," he said. "And sorry about before."

"Before?"

"Yeah, my language."

The girl stared at him. Then, slowly, a wide smile spread across her face. Without another word, she turned and went through the doors and down the hall.

Keith watched her until she turned the corner.

What the fuck?

Keith shook his head and went back into the lobby. He was halfway to the desk when the phone rang again. He jogged around the counter and picked up the receiver.

"Front desk, this is..."

"I know who the hell it is. I just told you there was someone screaming in the goddamn hallway and you didn't do a damn thing about it."

Keith pulled the phone away from his ear and stared at it in disbelief.

"Sir, I'm sorry. I just checked the hallway, and I didn't hear anything. Could you check your room number for me again? Perhaps you said the wrong number by mistake, and I checked the wrong hall?"

"It's 62," the man shouted. "I'm not stupid."

Keith felt his face burning. "I wasn't suggesting that at all, sir. I will take care of this."

"You better," the man said before ending the call.

Keith put the phone back on the cradle and ran his fingers through his hair. *What the hell is happening here?*

He let out a deep breath and pulled the radio from his pocket.

"Hank, you copy?"

Ten seconds passed before the radio chirped back.

"Yeah. What's up?"

"I just got my ass chewed by a guest. He called in a noise complaint, but there's nothing going on. I get back to the desk and he calls back, screaming at me for not taking care of it."

"That's not good," Hank said. "What room?"

"It's room 62. I asked him to double check when he called back. He was adamant."

"That's it, then. 62 is empty. He's got the wrong room number."

"You sure?"

"Check the guest log if you don't believe me. I'm sure. There are only seven rooms checked out tonight. That's not one of them."

Keith pulled up the guest list on the computer and saw Hank was right. Room 62 was empty, along with every room past it down the hall.

"You're right. So, what do I do? I don't know what room the guy is actually in?"

"Well, if you checked the east wing and got nothing, then I would check the west wing. Maybe he's in 26? Could've looked at his key card wrong?"

Keith nodded. "Good call," he said.

"I'd get on it quickly though, boss. Sounds like you don't want this guy calling back again."

"For sure," Keith answered. "I'm on it."

"Let me know how it goes," Hank added.

Keith put the radio in his pocket and made his way down the spiral stairs to the lower level. He glanced to his right toward the darkened dining room but saw nothing out of the ordinary. He went left, passing the closed heavy wooden doors of the lounge, and grabbed the handle of the glass doors to the west hall but stopped short of pushing it open.

Through the glass, he could see the girl from before standing at the branch of the hallway. She was staring at him with the same wide smile she had given him in the game room. The hairs on Keith's arms stood on end and goosebumps rippled across his skin.

The sound of the front desk phone ringing from above broke his gaze and he let his hand fall from the door handle. He turned and sprinted back up the stairs to the desk, his mind swirling with uncertainty.

"Front desk, this is Keith speaking."

"Hi Keith, it's me again. Just wondering if you've had any luck with my noise complaint?"

Dumbfounded, Keith stared at the phone. There was no anger or frustration in the man's voice at all. He sounded almost cheerful.

"Sir, I'm afraid you must be mistaken about your room number," Keith said. "Room 62 is empty tonight."

The man chuckled into the receiver, sending a fresh wave of chills down Keith's spine.

"Oh, it's 62, all right. It's always 62."

Something is not right here.

"Would you like to see my room, Keith?" asked the man. "You can hear them scream from here. Loud enough to wake the dead. You'll see, Keith."

Keith slammed the phone down onto the receiver. An involuntary gasp escaped his lips, and he sagged backward against the wall.

What the fuck is happening?

His heart pounded in his chest and dizziness washed over him in waves.

A voice spoke from the desk, causing Keith to cry out in alarm. Horrified, he tracked the voice to his cell phone on the counter. The audio player was still displayed on the screen, and the voice of the narrator had begun again.

"We've come to an important moment in our story. What the young man does now may very well decide his fate. Will he confront the menace in room 62? Will he challenge the smiling woman wherever she may be? Or is there another way? Does salvation await outside, or will the night only take him deeper into this tangled web of madness? Time will tell. Though I don't think the young man should delay his decision too long. Something is coming."

Keith felt the contents of his stomach liquify. A wave of nausea racked him, and he dropped to one knee by the small trash can behind the counter. He closed his eyes and breathed quick, shallow breaths. Slowly, the need to vomit faded away.

This can't be real. It can't be real. His thoughts whirled. How was this happening? This was no podcast. The narrator knew everything that had happened. He was being watched.

Keith pulled the radio from his pocket and pressed the button.

"Hank," he croaked. "What is happening? The podcast, I don't understand."

He waited, staring at the radio. There was no response.

"Hank, goddammit, what is this?"

The radio remained silent.

Keith put his forearm on the desk and pulled himself back to his feet. The woman stood directly in front of him with her arms crossed over the counter, an unnaturally wide smile stretched across her face.

"I know where the noise is coming from, Keith," she said. "Room 62. It's some party in there. People are dying to get in!"

She threw her head back and shrieked with laughter so loud that Keith instinctively covered his ears. With a cry of despair, he ran out from behind the counter and raced toward the main doors of the lobby. The automatic sensor had barely opened a gap for him to pass as his body slammed into the glass. Behind him, he could hear the woman laughing. Impossibly, it seemed to only get louder. He did not dare to look back.

Outside, the cool air whipped against his face as he sprinted down the stone path away from the hotel. He banked left and tore into the grass. He had to get to Hank. The pool was behind the hotel's east wing. He only hoped Hank was still there.

He was nearing the end of the building when a flash of light caught his attention. The curtain covering the glass patio door of one of the guest rooms was open. A man stood there wearing only boxer shorts. His torso was covered in blood streaming from deep lacerations on his chest. Keith slowed to a stop and stared. Even from this distance, he could see the number 62 savagely carved into his chest, glistening as the blood seeped from the wounds. The man raised the knife he held and tapped his forehead in a macabre salute. Keith screamed and stumbled on down the lawn.

Rounding the end of the building, Keith saw the white slats of the deck fencing around the hotel's in-ground pool. He searched frantically around the perimeter for any sign of Hank, but saw no one. A desperate groan escaped his lips.

"I'm over here, Keith," a voice said.

Keith snapped his head toward the hotel to see Hank sitting on a bench near the walking path around the grounds. He wore jeans and a blue button-up maintenance shirt. His toolbox sat next to him on the bench. Keith staggered toward Hank with tears burning in his eyes.

"What is this, Hank?" he sobbed. "What did you make me do?"

"I'm sorry, Keith. I truly am," Hank said. He sighed and shook his head. "I've been here a long time, and this never gets easier."

Keith dropped to his knees in front of the bench. "Why?"

"It's this damned place. There's something evil here. Every so often, it needs to be fed."

"What the fuck are you talking about?" Keith screamed. "This is a public resort. There are people here all the time. Nobody else knows about the ghosts fucking with people?"

"They're not ghosts," Hank said. "They're what they need to be. Whatever it takes to scare you. Your fear, desperation, anxiety — it's all energy. Nectar of the gods."

Keith shook his head desperately. "No. This isn't real."

"I'm afraid it is. The time has come around again. Sometimes it's a housekeeper, or a busboy. Even a guest from time to time. Doesn't matter," Hank said. "Just has to be someone."

"I just want to go home," Keith said through tears.

"It's too late. When you pressed play on that podcast, you started a chain of events that cannot be undone. You engaged it. You woke it up."

"You told me to do it, you son of a bitch," Keith shouted.

"It's my job, Keith. Same as it was my old man's job, and my grandpa before that. Even before the hotel was here. This ground is marked. We were chosen to serve, to maintain the balance."

Keith scrambled to his feet and staggered away. "I'm leaving, and you can't stop me. They can't stop me either," he said, gesturing toward the hotel. "I'm outside now. They can't get me out here."

"It's like I said, it's not the hotel. It's the ground. Doesn't matter if you're inside or outside. The reach is long." Slowly, Hank lifted a hand and pointed to the trees.

Keith turned, and his stomach churned into an icy slush. The girl stood just beyond the tree line, leering at him with that hideous smile.

"You'd better run," she called out in a menacing sing-song melody. "I'm coming!"

The girl launched herself into a sprint and raced toward him, her maniacal laughter echoing off the forest. In desperation, Keith ran back to the hotel. He looked helplessly at Hank as he passed, but the old maintenance man had closed his eyes and bowed his head.

Rather than run back around the building, he angled toward the center of the resort. There was a deck off the dining room, and he prayed the door inside would be unlocked. The girl's laughter mocked him as he ran, but did not sound as if it were getting any closer.

The wooden staircase up to the deck level came into view and Keith rocketed up, taking two steps at a time. He darted across the deck, weaving through tables with closed umbrellas anchored in the centers, and grabbed the door handle. Much to his relief, it turned easily, and the door swung open. As he ran inside, his mind registered that he could no longer hear the girl laughing, but the adrenaline surging through him did not allow time to ponder what that might mean.

Emerging into the darkened dining room, he allowed himself to slow for a second, gasping for air. His lungs burned, and he felt dizzy. Just as he reached the front counter, a high-pitched *CHING* sounded, stopping him in mid-step. He spun wildly and sobbed when he saw her. The girl sat at one of the dining room tables along the railing. She held a wineglass in one hand and a fork in the other.

"Excuse me, sir, but I've been waiting forever for a refill!"

Keith screamed at her in despair and stumbled out of the dining room. The spiral staircase loomed ahead, and he pushed himself harder. If he could get back upstairs and out the front again, maybe he could get to his car and get away. Maybe he could beat the devil yet.

He climbed the staircase quickly, keeping an eye on the darkened hallway below, but the girl did not appear. The warm light of the lobby gave him a brief sense of relief, a glimmer of hope missing in the darkness. Immediately, the illusion crumbled when he turned toward the front desk to grab his keys. The girl stood behind the counter with the front desk phone pressed to her ear. She now wore a Terra Bay uniform. The gold name tag on her chest glittered in the light, and Keith felt all the fight drain from him. The name tag read *Inevitable*.

"Front desk," she said. "What's that? There is a crazy man running around the resort? Oh, my! I will take care of it right away. He'll be dead soon. Please enjoy the rest of your stay!"

Keith turned away from her, numb and defeated, and staggered back through the game room and into the guest wing. Tears were falling freely, and he had lost all reasoning power. Instinct told him to flee the girl, and he blindly followed. He whimpered softly as he rounded the corner. Halfway down the hall, he heard the emergency exit door open in front of him. He didn't have to look up to know who it was. Keith stopped, closed his eyes, and waited for the end to come. He listened for her footsteps to come charging at him, but instead he heard the guest room door beside him creak open. He turned to look at the gold plate by the door, though he knew what it would say.

62

"Come see my room, Keith," the man said. "Come hear the screams."

He reached out a blood-soaked fist and grabbed Keith's shirt, jerking him into the room. The door slammed shut, but not before the screams began.

Hank Allen walked up the spiral stairs into the hotel lobby and crossed over to the front desk. He sat down in the chair and picked up Keith's cell phone. As he did, a voice sounded from the speaker.

"We've reached the end of our tale. The young man found out there was much more than meets the eye in this hotel. The evil that lurks within is satisfied, for a time. Now, it will rest. Until next time."

The audio file ended, and the phone screen went black. Hank didn't bother trying to turn it back on. He knew the phone was fried. He dropped it into his shirt pocket to dispose of later.

"Until next time."

MAX BET

B lane Townsend gazed at the glowing screen of the slot machine in front of him. He clutched a nearly empty beer can in his left hand, and the palm of his right hand rested on the machine panel with his fingers hovering over a button marked Spin Again. He glanced up at the graphics on the tall screen. Three stone monoliths stood amongst a sandy desert background. A cartoon Cleopatra smiled at him from the top corner. The monoliths were color coded, and the center tower was one green block away from triggering a chance to spin for the jackpot.

He looked back down at the bottom of the screen. 380 credits. $3.80. Gently, he placed a finger on the button for a max bet of $3.50.

Fuck it.

He smacked the button and leaned back in the stool, inhaling deeply as the pictures whirled around the animated wheel. When they stopped, random jumbles of Egyptian caricatures and hieroglyphs alerted him he was not a winner.

"Dammit," he muttered under his breath.

He slapped a button labeled Collect, and a voucher emerged from the machine. He snatched it up and looked at the thirty cents balance. In a fit of anger, he crumpled up the paper and threw it. The wad sailed three machines down the aisle where it bounced off the head of an old woman with a walker next to her stool.

"Watch it, asshole!" she shouted, before turning back to her own game.

"I'm sorry," Blane replied, though the woman was not listening.

I gotta get out of here.

He got to his feet and navigated his way towards the front of the casino. The place was packed, even for a Friday night. People laughed and shouted around him. A live band played at the central bar. There were no card tables or roulette wheels, only slot machines, but the nearest full-fledged casino was two hours away. In rural Ohio, you took what you could get.

Two attendants in dark suits stood by the exit as Blane walked past. He glanced towards them and nodded.

"Enjoy the rest of your evening, sir," the taller of them said.

Fat fucking chance there, pal.

Cold air greeted him as he stepped outside. Valet parking attendants scurried around the front drive. He crossed the road and jogged across the parking lot until he found his car. He fumbled in his pocket for the key, hit the unlock button, and dropped into the seat. The quiet inside the car was a stark contrast to the incessant buzz of the casino, and he welcomed the change.

He pulled his phone from his pocket and the screen lit up, revealing a picture of Jules and Benji. A pang of guilt racked his stomach at the sight of them. His beautiful wife and their wonderful baby boy. They depended on him to support them, and here he was fucking it all up.

Reluctantly, he swiped the screen until he saw the icon for the bank app. Filled with dread, he typed in his password and hit submit. The loading screen flashed, the account summary page popped, and Blane gasped.

How many times did I go to the ATM?

"Oh fuck," he whispered.

According to the app, there was only seventy-six dollars left in the checking account. Blane thought he might vomit.

How did I let this happen?

Even as he thought the words, they rang hollow in his mind. He knew damn well how this happened. He was addicted. How someone could go from regular guy to gambling addict in less than two months was beyond him, but here he was. The first night had gotten him. On a whim, Blane and Jules had gone to the casino for a once in a blue moon date night. They set a limit of fifty dollars each they were comfortable losing. After wandering the floor and taking in the sights, they settled down to a pair of machines next to each other. Blane fed a twenty into the machine, set the minimum bet, and let it spin. Five minutes later, he was up two hundred and fifty dollars. Jules clung to his arm and laughed every time the machine lit up. He was winning at a ridiculous rate, and it felt amazing. It was a rush. That first high, and he'd been chasing it ever since.

That had been seven weeks ago. Since then, Jules had gone back with him a couple times, but they always left with less money than they came with.

"Can't win all the time," she said on one of those quiet trips home. "If everybody won every time they went, they'd go out of business."

As the thrill of that first night faded further, Jules lost interest in going. Blane couldn't turn it off. It was like an itch in the back of his mind all the time. If he could just get back there and find the right machine, find the one that spoke to him, he knew he could hit a big one.

So that was what he'd been doing every chance he got. Twice a week, he headed to the casino after work. Those nights, he told Jules he was working late. He hated lying to her, but he knew she wouldn't approve of what he was doing. He formed a twisted logic that he was doing this for them. They weren't in terrible shape financially, but it could be better. If he could hit a few thousand dollars on a low-level jackpot, that would be a game changer for them. He knew he could do it. He felt it. The big hit was coming.

Now he was in trouble. The seventy-six dollar balance on his phone was a red alert. The electric, water, and cable bills were all due in the next week. He had gone into the casino with $600 in the account, enough to cover the bills and a couple hundred to spare. He was just hoping to double up that extra and maybe he could take Jules out for a special date night.

I'm so fucked.

He thought about Jules. She would be curled up on the couch in her pjs watching tv with Benji asleep in her lap. She was probably checking her phone every few minutes, hoping to see an "I'm on my way home" text from him.

"FUCK!!!" he roared. He slapped the dashboard in unison with his outbursts. "FUCK, FUCK, FUCK!"

What could he possibly say to her? Hey babe, can you ask your parents for some money to cover our bills because I gambled all of ours away? That would go over well. The worst part was she would do it. She loved him, and they would work through it. They were a family, and she wouldn't let a mistake ruin the whole thing. He could imagine the hurt but accepting look in her eyes as she hugged him and told him it was okay. It felt like failure, and he couldn't let it go down that way. He knew what he had to do.

He looked at the bank app one more time. Seventy-six dollars wouldn't pay the bills anymore than zero dollars would.

"Lady luck, I need you now."

Before he could change his mind, he flung open the car door and made for the main entrance. It was a clear night and the nearly full moon glowed. He looked up at the stars as he crossed the parking lot. *I need this now.*

He pulled open one of the tall, glass front doors and the sights and sounds assaulted his senses. The attendant who had wished him a good evening watched him pass through the entry checkpoint.

"Welcome back, sir."

Blane gave him another quick nod, but this time he noticed the hint of a smirk on the man's face. Blane felt his own face flush red, but he kept his mouth shut and waded into the crowd of people.

In the short time he was outside, the casino seemed to have gotten even busier. Blane couldn't move more than a few feet without having to stop or sidestep to avoid running into someone. He scanned the rows of slot machines as he worked his way across the floor. The few open machines did not catch his attention.

He waited in a short line at the ATM. When it was his turn, he popped his bank card into the machine and input the pin number. The machine only dispensed cash in $20 increments, so he tapped the $60 icon on the screen. The now familiar screen alerted him this machine would charge a $6.50 bank fee. Blane rolled his eyes and acknowledged that he accepted the fee.

Another pass through the crowded floor yielded similar results. He would not settle for any open machine. It had to be the right one. He found himself at the back end of the building. From here, the sound of the house band diminished to only the dull thump of the bass drum.

"You lookin' for a hot one?" asked a voice in his ear.

Blane turned and froze as his eyes landed on the woman behind him. She was a knockout. Long red hair bounced around her bare shoulders.

A tight black dress framed her body and tied behind her neck. She smiled at Blane and let his eyes linger for a moment before she spoke again.

"I said, are you looking for a hot one?"

"I'm sorry," Blane replied. "I'm just playing the slots."

The girl smirked at Blane before letting out a laugh. "Honey, I wasn't referring to myself. What kind of girl do you think I am?"

Blane's face turned an alarming crimson color. "I didn't mean…"

"Shhh," she whispered, putting a finger to Blane's lips. "Do you hear that?"

Blane gently shook his head, her finger dragging across his lips. Despite everything, Jules popped into his head and he felt his stomach turn with guilt. He had done nothing wrong, and yet he felt like he was breaking rules.

"I hear a winner," she said. "I think that's what you're looking for, Blane. I think that's what you need."

"How do you know my name?"

"The same way I know you have $60 in your pocket you can't afford to lose."

Blane flinched at the accuracy of her claim.

"Have you been following me? Who are you?"

"I don't need to follow anyone. I'm Lucy, and right now I think you need me a lot more than I need you."

Blane frowned. A mild dizziness flowed through him, and he gave an exaggerated shake of his head to clear his mind.

"I don't understand. Why would I need you?"

Lucy leaned into him and put her lips against his ear. "Because I hear a winner, and you need me to show you."

Goosebumps broke out all over Blane as the heat of her breath pressed against his face. An almost overwhelming smell of cinnamon drifted off her.

"Tell me I'm wrong," she whispered.

Blane swallowed hard.

"You're not wrong."

"Then follow me."

Lucy took his hand and pulled him back into the rows of slot machines. Blane followed along, peering at the other casino patrons around them. No one made eye contact with him. No one stared after Lucy as she moved through the crowd. Confusion filled his mind, but in the forefront was Jules. He knew she was miles away in their apartment, but he half expected to see her standing there in the casino, arms crossed, as he let this strange woman lead him across the room.

What the hell am I doing?

"Only what you need to do," Lucy said. She looked over her shoulder at him and smiled mischievously.

Blane felt the color drain from his face.

"Did you read my mind?"

Lucy winked at him, but said nothing.

As they neared the opposite wall of the casino, she changed course and pulled him to a stop in front of an open slot machine. The digital screen flashed red and yellow. Slender red devils with extravagant black mustaches danced around the screen.

"This is the one," Lucy said. She put a hand on Blane's shoulder and pushed him towards the stool. "This is where you get it all back, and so much more."

Blane let her guide him into the seat. The last few minutes had been surreal. There were people everywhere, and yet Blane felt like he and

Lucy were the only ones there. It was as if she had created a force field around them, and the rest of the patrons were oblivious to their presence.

Lucy snapped her fingers in front of his face, bringing him to attention. "You're wasting time, Blane. You don't want her to stop singing, do you? Not before you get what you need."

Blane slid a hand into his pocket and pulled out the twenties, but found he couldn't take his gaze from Lucy. He stared into her green eyes and watched as slivers of red and orange flashed around the iris like flame.

She leaned towards him and put her lips against his ear. Again, the smell of cinnamon engulfed him and the hairs on his arms stood up as the heat of her breath caressed his ear.

"Play," she whispered.

Blane swiveled the stool back around and inserted the sixty dollars into the machine. Bells and whistles sounded off as the game credit jumped to 6000. The now familiar adrenaline rush that accompanied a fresh start on the machines filled his veins. He set a mid-level bet and tapped the Spin button.

The slots whirled. When they stopped, three devils with pitchforks remained. A spider web of lines connected all the winning combinations, and the machine declared an $18.22 hit.

"Yes," Blane whispered. It was the first hit of any significance he'd had all night. Getting a win was a weight off his shoulders. He felt alive again.

Lucy stood behind him with a long-fingered hand draped across the back of the stool. "That was just a tease," she said. "Are you gonna play this thing or not?"

Blane turned and looked up at her with glazed eyes.

"Max out that bet," Lucy said. "If you want to hit big, bet big."

"Max bet," Blane replied in a slurred voice. He felt like he was in a hole and everything was a million miles away.

He turned back around and switched to the maximum bet of $7.50. He cringed a little. This was a higher priced machine than he would normally play.

The first few spins came up empty. He panicked as his credits dropped $7.50 every shot.

"Don't hold back, Blane. She's singing so loud. Don't you hear it? She's ready to blow."

Blane heard nothing save the hum of conversations that seemed to echo from another place. Still, he nodded and pressed on. Max bet after max bet. His anxiety grew sharper with every losing spin.

Finally, he stopped and pushed himself away from the machine. The last spin had dropped him below $9 of credit. He glared up at Lucy.

"I don't hear any singing, and I'm losing my ass here. You said you could help me."

"You're so close, Blane," she replied. "So very close. She sings so loud it could split the sky. I'll show you."

She reached out and touched a cherry red fingernail against his temple. Blane felt a sharp sting as she dug in and scraped down. A drop of blood emerged from the abrasion and Blane gasped.

Instantly, the casino shifted to a crimson hue. A high-pitched wailing blasted his senses, and he desperately clapped his hands over his ears. All around him, the casino patrons were thrashing wildly in their stools. Two machines to his left, a man was bashing his face into the monitor repeatedly. A woman at the next machine ripped clumps of hair from her own head and shoved them into her mouth as tears of blood streaked her face. The live band continued to play at the center bar across the room, but they now held new instruments. The drummer pounded his kit with severed arms. The guitarist and bass players both wore guitars fashioned from human torsos. The woman at center stage was the source of the wailing vocals. She was nude, and the crowd gathered at the edge of the stage repeatedly swiped at her with curved blades. Blood streaked over her body, but she continued to sing the shrieking song, not reacting to the wounds.

Blane stared in horror at the madness and carnage unfolding around him. He tried to stand up, but two red hands shoved him back onto the stool. He looked up to see Lucy. Her skin now matched the red of her hair, and two black horns protruded from her forehead. Like the woman on the stage, she was now nude as well. Black and gold swirls decorated her body, wrapping up her legs, across her hips, around her breasts, and over her shoulders. She climbed onto the stool and straddled Blane. Her skin was hot against his. Blane stared into her eyes, which were now a stark yellow that no longer hinted at flames, but had become a living inferno.

"One more spin, and you'll have everything you want. Your worries will end. Give yourself to me, and you will have your wish. You will be mine, but that's not so bad, is it?" She pressed herself forward and buried Blane's face into her chest.

Blane struggled and twisted his face away from her. The heat from her skin took his breath. As he turned away, he saw the security guard at the front of the casino staring at him. In place of his suit, he now wore nothing but chains that shackled him to the floor. His body was a landscape of atrocities. His face was wet with tears and he pleaded to Blane through anguished eyes. Frantically, he shook his head back and forth, desperate to dissuade Blane.

Lucy took Blane by the chin and jerked his face back towards her. She hissed and revealed a forked tongue. She leaned in against him and ran a forked tongue across the blood trickling from the abrasion on his head. Blane flinched against the sting and heard a sizzling sound followed by a snap.

He blinked rapidly a few times as the bright lights of the casino returned. Around him, everything had returned to normal. Lucy stood next to him and smiled deviously.

"What's it gonna be?" she asked. "You can spin one more time and that machine is going to light up like fireworks. Jules can have all the things you want to give her. The price is you will belong to me. Or you can collect your $8 and go home. I'm sure Jules will understand. Deep down, she knows you're a failure. It won't surprise her you blew it. It's your decision, Blane. Make the call."

Blane looked at her and then looked at the slot machine. He thought of Jules and Benji, imagined the look on her face when he told her what happened. He thought of the security guard at the front entrance with chains locked around his neck, and the barrage of violence and atrocities he had seen.

He made the call.

Jules woke to the sound of the apartment door opening. She rubbed sleep from her eyes and checked her phone to see it was nearly 1:00 am. Benji was sound asleep in the bassinet beside the couch. She tucked the blankets in around him and softly ran a finger across his hair.

She walked down the hall towards the kitchen and found Blane standing at the counter with a bottle of beer in his hand.

"Where have you been?" she asked sleepily. "You worked this late?"

"Sorry, babe," he replied. "I should've called, but I was afraid I would wake you or Benji."

He took a long pull from his bottle of beer.

"It was a good night, though. I had a business meeting with a potential client at the casino, believe it or not. Looks like I'm going to be working with them on some projects."

"That's awesome! Wonder if they'll give us any free plays?"

Blane chuckled. "Funny you say that. I played a few spins while I was there, and you won't believe what I hit."

THOSE THAT HELP THEMSELVES

The man burst into the room, slamming the door into the wall. Picture frames rattled and threatened to fall to the wooden floor of the cabin. Panting heavily, he grabbed the knob and pushed the door closed, collapsing his considerable weight against it. There were blood smears across the front of his blue and gray checked flannel shirt. As he rested and struggled to catch his breath, he could hear muffled whimpering coming from the girl in the room behind him.

"Dear God, what have I done?"

He moaned in desperation and pushed himself upright. A mirror on the opposite wall caught his attention. The face staring back at him was wild and disheveled. A deep scratch from the corner of his eye disappeared into his black, scruffy beard. He reached up and gently touched the wound, wincing at the sting of contact. His fingers came away wet and red.

"Oh no," he whimpered. "I've done it now. How will I explain this?"

He staggered across the room and dropped into a rickety kitchen chair. The chair legs swayed under him but held. Still panting, he surveyed the cabin. A small table was knocked over, and the large rug in the center of the room was pulled up and rolled over onto itself.

In his mind, he could see himself carrying the girl into the cabin. She thrashed frantically, and one of her kicks sent the end table crashing to the floor. She reached a clawed hand up and swiped at his face. One long fingernail took hold just below his eye and sliced. He cried out and twisted away, then nearly fell as he tripped on the rug and dragged it halfway across the room.

The man rocked steadily back and forth in his seat, replaying the events in his mind. At last, he had gotten her through the doorway and into the small bedroom. Then he had done things to her, terrible things.

"Oh Jesus, what have I done!" he cried out to the empty room.

He could hear the girl sobbing from behind the closed door, though the gag he tied around her head muffled the noise.

The chair creaked as he sprang to his feet and began pacing around the room. The cabin was small. A living room area and small kitchen formed an L shape around the single bedroom. A closet sized bathroom completed the floor plan. It had been years since the man had been out here. His father bought the place when he retired from the steel mill. For a time, it was a regular weekend getaway for their family. When his father passed, his mother signed the cabin over to him. He brought his wife out a few times when they were newlyweds, but she was a city girl and cared very little for the scenic beauty of the forest. After the last disastrous weekend, he gave up on romantic trips to the cabin. But he thought about it an awful lot. In his mind, it had become a hideaway. It was a place where he could do things without the world watching, like the things he'd done to the girl.

Again, he cried out to the empty room as what he'd done replayed in his mind. He grabbed a handful of hair with both hands and yanked. He walked to the front door and dropped his forehead against the wood. He felt like crying. Then he stiffened at the sound of a motor. He dashed across the room to the window. The road was a good fifty yards away and thick trees blocked any view of the cabin, but he panicked, nonetheless.

What if someone saw me take her? They could've called the cops or followed me here.

He stared at the gravel driveway curving through the trees and waited for the police car to come tearing at him. Slowly, he allowed himself to relax a bit as the sound of the motor faded away and no one came. He scanned the area surrounding the cabin for anyone on foot. His eyes stopped on the back of his car and his stomach lurched.

"The fucking trunk!" he shouted.

The trunk of his beat-up Cavalier stood wide open, and even from this distance, he could see the blood smears on the taillight covers.

The man raced out of the cabin and crossed the small patch of yard, dry leaves crunching under his boots. He reached into the open trunk and pulled out an oil-stained rag. He frantically wiped the blood off the taillights, horrified by the handprints she left behind while being dragged from the trunk.

When he was satisfied, he closed the lid and trudged back to the cabin. The oil rag was now dark red. *Have to burn it,* he thought. He was defeated. The adrenaline he felt previously was long gone. In its place was a looming dread. His world collapsing around him. He would go to prison. Everyone he knew would abandon him.

The man entered the cabin, closed the door softly behind him, and dropped onto the couch. He could still hear whimpering from the bedroom, but it was softer now. This made him feel even worse, and he began to cry himself. Loud, bellowing sobs filled the small building.

Eventually, he regained control of himself. He wiped his eyes and pulled the phone from his pocket. A text message from his wife read, "Hope you're having a good time fishing. Catch the big one!"

He shook his head and cleared the alert. He couldn't think about her right now. Right now, needed help. As great as she was, she couldn't help him with this. She wouldn't understand.

He swiped the screen until the familiar YouTube app appeared. He touched the icon and went straight to his subscribed channels. The one he needed was at the top of the list. The channel was called Becoming the Best You. A blue dot on the page icon showed a new video.

"Thank God," he whispered and tapped the screen once more to start the newly uploaded video.

A pretty blond girl in workout attire jogged down a suburban street. In the background, kids played in front yards, a man sprayed down his car with a water hose, and an old couple walked hand in hand on the sidewalk. The phone jostled from side to side as she ran, causing the video to bounce with each step.

"Hey guys!" she said excitedly to the camera. "Welcome to another episode of Becoming the Best You! In case this is your first time joining us, my name's Britney and I've been helping people just like you unlock their potential and become a better version of themselves."

The man smiled and nodded at the phone.

"The first step is knowing your own heart," she continued. "Whatever the thing is inside you that gets you fired up and excited, that is what you have to go after. There are all kinds of reasons that people don't chase their dreams. They think it will never happen. What will people think of me if I do this? How will society look at me if I step outside the box they think I belong in? Does that sound familiar?"

"Yes," the man answered. His eyes were wide and unblinking as the girl continued her jog.

"Well, I've got news for you. What other people think about what you're doing DOESN'T MATTER! This is YOUR life, and you live it

YOUR way. No matter how crazy your dream is, no matter what the thing is that you need to do to make yourself whole, go out there and get it. Face those fears, do the things that push you out of your comfort zone. Do the things that other people say you can't do, or you shouldn't do. Be true to yourself and everything else will fall into place."

The jogging girl hypnotized him. His knee bounced in rhythm with her steps, and he nodded enthusiastically.

"That's the lesson for today, and I'm going to give you a little home-work this time. I want you to think of something that you've always wanted to do, but were afraid to do it. Then I want you to take the first step towards achieving that goal. Just the first step. I think you'll find that once you've taken that first step, each step after that will get easier and easier, and before you know it, you're running as fast as you can to the BEST YOU!!!"

A huge smile lit up the man's face.

"Until next time, keep working and doing all the things that make you happy. With every step you are BECOMING THE BEST YOU! Bye!"

The video ended, and the man let out a deep sigh. He scrolled down to the comments section of the video, tapped the box, and typed.

Britney,

I am a huge fan of your channel and I just want you to know that you are helping people. I was afraid to chase my dreams because of what everyone would think. You've taught me it doesn't matter what people think, and I have to live for myself. So, I am doing it. I'm doing all the things I've thought about but never did. I'm doing it, and it's all because of you. Thank you so much for helping me BECOME THE BEST ME!!!

Feeling rejuvenated, he stood and put the phone back in his pocket. He walked to the bedroom door and pushed it open. The girl was where he had left her, wrists tied to the iron headboard. Her feet were loose, and she pulled herself into a tight ball. She had worked out of the gag, which now hung limply around her neck. She stared up at him with terror in her eyes.

"Please let me go," she begged. Despite her fear, she held his gaze. "Why are you doing this?"

The man smiled at her. "I'm chasing my dreams," he replied. He turned and closed the bedroom door behind him before turning his attention back to her. As he spoke, he pulled the hunting knife from his back pocket and flipped open the blade.

"Don't you see? I'm becoming the best me."

GONE FISHIN'

Jim McKinney cast out his line. The lure made a soft *plunk* as it hit the surface and disappeared into the water. The sun had broken the tree line to the east, covering the lake in brilliant shades of red and yellow. A soft breeze swept across the water, wrapping Jim in the cool touch of a June morning. It would have been perfect if not for the smell. Despite his best efforts, he could not escape the stench of rot.

The dead people standing along the bank were multiplying constantly. In some places, they were shoulder to shoulder. He couldn't see the north bank, but he suspected he would find the same if he bothered to fire up the troll motor and investigate. He was surrounded, so no matter which way the wind blew, he was bombarded by the smell of decaying flesh.

Three days prior, it had not been so bad. A few of the dead were loitering around the ramp as he backed the trailer into the water. He smashed one in the head with a crowbar when it ventured too close while he worked to release the boat. All the supplies he would need were already on the boat, and he left the truck parked on the ramp. He had no plans to return to it, and the odds of anyone else trying to back in were incredibly slim.

The first night was peaceful, disturbed only by the occasional groan from one of the creatures. By the second night, the bank was alive with a constant movement as more and more of them reached the edge. On the third night, there was no question. He wasn't getting out of the water alive.

Fucking zombies.

At first, the news coverage had referred to them as "infected". In less than a day, the word "zombie" was trending on social media. It was as good a word as any, and the parallels between what actually happened and the plot of a hundred horror movies were eerily similar. The first reports were labeled as random acts of violence by people under the influence of some contaminated strain of street drug. Within days, the cities became war zones, and no area of the country was unscathed. News reports became frantic outbursts with vague instructions to reach safety until there were no safe places to go. The world burned to the ground, and it only took three weeks.

Jim reeled in his line, checked the lure, and cast it out again.

Plunk.

As he slowly cranked the rod, he thought about Cheryl and the boys. He'd thought about them a lot. The boys were grown, living their own lives. Garrett was a truck driver. He was hauling a trailer out west when it started. Peyton was a high school teacher in Cincinnati. He hoped they were okay. In his heart, he knew they were not.

It was one thing to suspect that his sons were gone, victims of this damn nightmare the world had turned into. It was another thing altogether to know that Cheryl was gone. He saw her life taken from her by one of those monsters. Then he had seen the undead version of her fall. He'd taken care of that himself.

For a time, their home in rural Ohio had proven to be a haven. They were miles from the nearest town, most of those quite small, and only a few neighbors to speak of. The house was stocked with supplies, and

Jim had a respectable arsenal stashed away. While civilization collapsed on television, their world remained mostly unchanged. Jim was retired and Cheryl worked from home, so it wasn't a stretch for them to stay put in the house. The biggest change was Jim couldn't jump in the truck and take the boat to the lake whenever he felt like it, which he felt like doing a lot.

Everything crashed to a halt that last morning when Cheryl went out to fetch the eggs. Jim had built a coop a few years back and raised around a dozen chickens, harvesting more eggs than they could need. Jim sat on the front porch, sipping a cup of coffee and scanning the countryside for any of the creatures. He had only seen a handful of them since the outbreak began, and even then, only from a distance. Looking back on it, the lack of zombies roaming the countryside had lulled him into a false sense of security. He should have known better. When Cheryl screamed, he knew exactly what had happened.

He jumped out of the glider on the porch, his coffee mug shattering on the wooden floor, and raced around the side of the house. Cheryl lay on the ground beside the chicken coop. A zombie was perched atop her, bent forward, tearing at her throat. An involuntary choking sound escaped him. Her still body left no doubt. She was dead.

The zombie, having heard Jim's choking sob, turned slowly toward him. Meat hung from the creature's mouth, and the fresh spray of blood from Cheryl's lacerated neck contrasted with the pale hue of the creature's skin. Slowly, it climbed to its feet and stumbled in Jim's direction.

Enraged, Jim sprinted at the zombie and tackled it. His eyes fell on a cinder block sitting on the ground next to the coop, and Jim yanked it up with one hand, pinning the monster down with the other. He raised the stone block above his head and drove it into the creature's face. The impact killed it instantly, shattering the skull and destroying the brain, but Jim continued to slam the block, again and again, until nothing remained but a pulpy ruin.

He rolled off the creature and lay on the grass. The sky was clear and the bright blue you only get in summer. To Jim, it felt like a mocking sense of normalcy compared to the surrounding carnage. He lay there for a few moments, waiting for some reaction to come. He felt like he should scream or cry. Instead, he felt numb. He might have stayed there in the grass forever, but Cheryl moved beside him. He saw her leg twitch in his peripheral vision, and he lurched up to a sitting position. There was a flicker of hope that maybe she was alright, but he extinguished it quickly. He had seen enough news reports to know what happened to people who were bitten.

He got to his feet, not daring to look at Cheryl for fear that seeing her open eyes would break him, and walked to the house. He pulled open the back screen door, stepped inside the kitchen, and grabbed the shotgun he left sitting there in case of an emergency, in case one of those things got too close to the house.

Cheryl was one of those things now.

A half full bottle of whiskey sat on the counter, and he snatched it up, took a long pull, then stepped back outside. Cheryl was on her feet and stumbling toward him. Before he could change his mind, he leveled the shotgun at her.

"I'm sorry, Cheryl."

The chickens erupted into a frenzy as the shotgun blast echoed.

Sometimes, even now out on the lake, the sound of the shotgun goes off in his head, reminding him of what he had to do.

He reeled his line back in, switched out the lure, and cast it back out.

Plunk.

The days following Cheryl's death were the darkest of his life. The bar he kept moderately stocked pre-zombies depleted quickly. Every waking minute was spent with a bottle in hand or near at hand. The other hand stayed close to his 9mm. His days blurred into a drunken delirium of alternating stares between the bottom of a bottle and the barrel of a gun. Jim had been naïve to think they would ride out the end of the world together right at home. Now he was alone and there was nothing left to live for.

The last day at the house started like the rest of the post-Cheryl days. He woke up to a relentless hangover, empty liquor bottles scattered around the house. His gun lay on the coffee table by the couch, always within reach. As he frequently did, he picked it up and held it in front of him; the barrel aimed at his face.

What am I waiting for?

He contemplated the question as if he didn't know the answer. It was the same answer every time he put the gun in his mouth or to his temple.

He was afraid.

The house was a tomb, and it was a matter of time before he succumbed to one form of self-annihilation or another. Either he would blow his brains out, or he would drink himself to death. There was no reason to stay, and yet there was nowhere to go.

That was when the lightbulb went off in his head. There was, in fact, somewhere to go. The same place he always wanted to go.

The lake.

Almost instantly, the plan fell into place in his mind. It was so absurd, yet so perfect. The simplicity of it sent him into a fit of laughter, aggravating his already severe headache. For the first time in days, he had a purpose. The final act of his story.

He loaded down the boat with all the bottled water and canned food he could fit, hooked the trailer to his truck, and pulled away for the last time. He glanced back at the house as he coasted down the driveway. In his mind, he imagined Cheryl standing on the porch, waving at him.

Three hours later, the boat was in the water. The trip normally took only an hour, but several detours to avoid abandoned cars on the road slowed him down. It was a scenic drive, which spared him from encountering too many of the dead. Mostly, they wandered into the fields and turned to watch him pass. In his rearview, he saw them change course and follow the fading sound of the motor. That sound turned out to be a beacon, he would come to realize. The scattered few zombies around the lake turned into an army over the course of three days he'd been on the water.

Jim's pole twitched, and he mechanically set the hook and reeled in a small bluegill. He removed the hook with a steady hand, then held the fish up in front of his face. He looked into the small eyes of the creature.

Living eyes.

It was a comfort to share a space, if only for a moment, with another living creature. He sighed and dropped the fish back into the lake and watched it disappear.

The zombies on the bank moaned and shuffled around, excited by Jim's heightened activity. He watched them with contempt. He felt like an animal in a zoo being gawked at by a horde of onlookers. He knew the more proper analogy was the dead were vultures, waiting for a wounded animal to die. Waiting to feed.

Curiously, the dead did not seem to like the water. Once, on the first day, one of them had walked into the lake towards him. It disappeared into the water and never resurfaced. Jim hypothesized that the thing's lungs had filled with water, causing it to sink, and it probably dropped into a deep area of the lake and couldn't get out. He found it disturbing to think about the dead man pacing around the bottom of the lake, in darkness, for who knew how long? Eternity?

Another horrifying scenario occasionally played through his mind where the dead would walk into the water, one by one, filling the lake with corpses on top of corpses, until his boat floated atop the dead and the last wave would walk on a dead sea and take him. It was an outlandish thought, but then again, the world had become an outlandish place.

Jim knew this wouldn't last forever. Eventually, he would run out of supplies. Eventually, he would run out of hope.

Eventually, he would use the gun one last time.

For now, though, he was fishing.

Plunk.

VICTIMS OF THE ELEMENTS

Ian Dedrich stared out the window of the research station at the blankets of frozen earth stretching out to the horizon. Snow drifts rose high into the air against hillsides. Aside from the occasional blip of exposed black rock, the landscape was a kaleidoscope of whites and blues glittering fiercely as rays of sunlight tried but failed to warm the surface.

He dropped his forehead against the window, wincing as the cold seeped through the pane, and closed his eyes. The glass was thick, but not thick enough to stop the howling sounds of the unrelenting arctic winds from creeping through and into his ears. To his delirious mind, it sounded like invisible beasts shrieking at the sky.

For eight days he had been alone. The Sherman Institute of Arctic Research had failed. His partners had fallen victim to the elements. One by one, they perished. Veronica was the last. He had seen the fear in her eyes as she took her last breaths.

For days, Ian radioed for help. Again, and again, the distress call had been sent. Only silence replied. Eventually, as the solitude frayed his mind, the silence became a voice unto itself. Sometimes, it was so loud Ian would drop to the floor, hands over his ears, and scream until his throat burned. The silence tormented him. It told lies that filled him with hope. The sound of a voice, the sound of rescue. Perhaps it was his mind that told him lies, tricked him into believing. Perhaps the silence and his mind had joined forces to entertain themselves in the absence of any stimulation.

Now, his head pressed firmly against the glass, the howling outside a welcome diversion to the pressing silence, he picked up a new sound. At first, he believed it to be another trick. The steady humming sound continued to approach, slowly morphing into a deep *WHOOMP, WHOOMP, WHOOMP.*

When he could no longer resist, he raised his head and opened his eyes. In the distance, a speck in the sky appeared. He had spent long hours staring out that window and was sure this object had not been there before. He stared hypnotically as the speck grew larger, more defined. Closer.

Before long, the image cleared enough for him to see the whirling blades atop the thing. The *WHOOMP* sound intensified to a roar. Snow lifted into the air as gushes of wind battered the ground, as if the gods were recalling the frozen death they had unleashed on this land. Ian gasped in unfiltered relief as the helicopter lowered to the ground.

Rescue.

He leapt to his feet, raced across the center room of the research center, and pulled open the door to his living quarters. The bodies of his companions were organized neatly. Heads were lined up along one shelf. Arms were stacked neatly in a pile in the corner. Legs, cut off mid-thigh, stood in a line along the wall. The remaining torsos were stacked, one atop the other, in the opposite corner. This was their resting place, where he had placed them.

Ian grabbed the fire axe leaning against the wall and carried it back into the center room. He positioned himself behind the door, axe at the ready. At last, the silence would be broken. The elements could be unleashed

again. Outside, he heard the unmistakable crunch of approaching footsteps in the snow.

Ian Dedrich smiled and waited.

FABRIC

My grandma Nancy taught me to sew when I was eight years old. She said it was becoming a lost art, and important I learn. Two or three days a week, she sat me down for an hour and worked with me. We started out learning to knit and crochet with yarn. I made mistakes, but she was always patient. Even when I'd throw my roll of yarn against the wall in frustration, she would only smile and encourage me.

"Now Lizzy, that won't get you anywhere," she would say. "Pick it up and start again."

"I'm just no good at this, Mama Nancy," I would answer back.

"No one is ever good at anything until they've done it enough. When you've done it enough, well then, it's like magic."

She said that a lot. Magic. I thought she wanted to make it seem more exciting. I know now that wasn't it at all.

Mama Nancy had lived with us for as long as I could remember. Grandpa Tom died not long after I was born, and Dad insisted Nancy move in. Our house was bigger than we needed for the three of us, so there was plenty of room for her. She had her own living area, bathroom, and even a small kitchenette. It also helped that she could babysit me when my parents worked long hours. Dad was a lawyer, and Mom was a college professor. In those years, I spent more time with her than I did with my parents, which was fine by me. Not that I didn't get along with my parents, they just didn't always have time for me. Mama Nancy always did.

By the time I was nine, I was making scarves, mittens, and even blankets. My parents would gush over how good I was, pulling out things I had made to show company. Mama Nancy would wink at me and smile.

Around this time, I graduated to needles and thread. This proved to be more painful. Countless times, I yelped as the needle punctured my finger. Mama Nancy would hand me a tissue to wipe up the blood and pat me on the arm. "It will get easier, dear."

And so it did. I developed calluses on my fingers, so it wasn't as easy to pierce the skin, and before long I wasn't poking myself anymore. After a few months of practice, I was making my own dresses out of flower printed fabric Mama Nancy bought for me. The girls at school would ask me where I got my dresses and then stare incredulously when I said I made them myself.

One summer afternoon, I was digging through Mama Nancy's sewing chest, trying to find a fresh roll of fabric. Near the bottom of the chest, my fingers dug into a silky texture I had never used before. I pulled it out to find a large quilt. It was beautiful. The silky material shimmered and reflected the lights in the room like nothing I had ever seen before.

"Don't you be cutting anything off that now, Lizzy," Mama Nancy said from behind me.

Startled, I dropped the blanket back into the chest and twirled around, my hands behind my back. I kept my eyes on the floor. I wasn't sure why, but I felt like she had caught me in the act of something mischievous.

Mama Nancy walked over and put a soft finger under my chin, tilting my face up to hers. "Now girl, you didn't do no wrong. That's just a special thing you had in your hands there."

She picked up the blanket, folded it up, and deposited it back into the chest.

"That's our family quilt. It's very special and very old."

"I'm sorry," I said. "I wasn't gonna cut it up or nothing. I was just looking. It's so pretty."

"It is pretty," she replied. "And I know you wouldn't cut anything up without asking first. You just caught me off guard, honey. One day, I'll pass it on to you. When you're ready."

"I'll take great care of it," I said.

Mama Nancy smiled, but even then, I could see a tired sadness in her eyes.

"I know you will, Lizzy."

It would be five years before I saw that quilt again.

I was a month removed from my fourteenth birthday, the day my mom stopped me after school. Her eyes were red rimmed and puffy, and I knew she had been crying.

"Your father had to have some tests done at the doctor," she said. "You know, for the headaches he's been having." A tear slid over her cheek and she wiped it away. "The scan showed a mass on his brain. They are keeping him at the hospital to run more tests, but it looks bad."

I didn't need her to say what it looked like. I had seen enough television shows and movies to know what it looked like.

Cancer.

She held my gaze for a moment before bursting into tears and pulling me into a fierce embrace. I could feel her tears soaking into my shirt.

When she regained control of herself, she grabbed me by the shoulders and kissed my forehead.

"Everything's going to be ok. The doctors will figure this out, and it will be fine."

I nodded, feeling my own tears well up.

"I'm going back to the hospital to meet your dad and talk with the doctors," she said. "You stay here with Nancy and I'll call as soon as I know something, ok?"

Again, I nodded. I was afraid if I made a sound, the tears I was barely containing would break free.

I watched her pull out of the driveway from the living room window. When she was out of sight, I turned and raced to the back of the house, to Mama Nancy. I didn't know what I needed, but I knew she could help.

Her bedroom door was closed, which was unusual, but I figured she was upset, too. I didn't bother knocking and barged into the room.

Mama Nancy was in her chair. All the blinds were closed, and candles were lit all around the room, causing shadows to dance on the walls. The family quilt was draped over her lap and she sewed furiously. I had never seen her hands work so fast. In and out, the needle looped through the silky fabric. She was muttering to herself and nodding her head in unison with the movement of the needle. In the flickering candlelight, I could see there was a long tear in the quilt.

I was so startled by the scene of her in the darkened room that for a moment I stood there transfixed. The image of her rocking back and forth, talking to herself as she frantically worked the needlepoint, was surreal.

"What happened?" I asked when I finally found my voice. "What happened to the quilt?"

Mama Nancy didn't answer. I don't think she knew I was there at all. She kept rocking and sewing, all the while muttering to herself. I strained my ears but could not make out the words.

"Mama Nancy? Are you okay?"

She tilted her head and cast a sideways glance at me, finally acknowledging my presence. There was a fire in her eyes I had never seen before. An intensity foreign to her usual peaceful exterior. I took an involuntary step back.

"Run along, girl," she said. "I'm awfully busy right now." She was looking at me, but her needle never slowed. "Run along."

I couldn't bring myself to speak, so I nodded tersely and backed out of the room. I closed the door gently and then ran as fast as I could to my room. By the time I reached my bed, tears were falling. I buried my face in the pillow and sobbed. Eventually, I fell asleep.

I woke to Mama Nancy gently shaking my shoulder. I sat up and rubbed sleep from my eyes. I could see through my bedroom window the sun had set and the last minutes of dusk were fading as the night took hold.

"Your mama is on the phone," she said. "She wants to talk to you."

The events of the afternoon flooded back into my mind, and the sick feeling in my stomach returned. I took the phone and tried to prepare myself for the news.

"Hi mom."

"Lizzy, you won't believe it! The doctors ran another scan, and the tumor is gone!"

"What?" I asked in disbelief. "How can that be?"

"I don't know. They said it could've been a malfunction on the first scan, but even they don't really know. It's a miracle, Lizzy," she said, laughing. "A miracle."

"That's amazing news," I said. It didn't seem real. The rollercoaster of emotions I had gone through over the last few hours left me feeling ragged and worn.

"We'll be home soon. We'll bring pizza."

"Ok, see you soon," I answered before hanging up the phone.

I looked up at Mama Nancy, who still stood beside the bed. She looked exhausted. The images of her in the candlelit bedroom, sewing feverishly lingered in my mind. She must have known what I was thinking. She reached out and ran a hand through my hair.

"I'll explain it to you soon, girl. Right now, you be happy your daddy's ok."

She left without another word.

When mom and dad got home, Mama Nancy didn't come down for dinner. I went up to her room to ask if she would like me to bring her anything. I found her in bed, sound asleep. A thought came to me then I couldn't resist. As quietly as I could, I tiptoed across the room and opened the chest. Laying on top was the family quilt. After glancing behind me to make sure she was still asleep, I pulled the blanket from the chest and let it unfold. I studied the fabric, letting it slide through my hands as I scanned it for the tear I had seen earlier. It was gone.

Mama Nancy moaned in her sleep and turned over. Quickly, I folded up the quilt and put it back in the chest. I tiptoed back across the room and closed her door gently behind me.

Even though I slept through the afternoon, I excused myself to bed early. I gave my dad a big hug and whispered in his ear, "I'm glad you're ok".

"Me too, honey," he said. "Me too."

I laid in bed with thoughts of hospitals and scans running through my mind. More than that, I thought about Mama Nancy and the quilt. I didn't sleep for a long time.

It would be nearly a month before I got the chance to talk to Mama Nancy about what happened. It felt like a secret between us, even though I didn't know what the secret was. Any time I felt like the time was right to bring it up, Mama Nancy would start up a new conversation and steer us in a different direction.

Finally, the day came that would present my opportunity. My parents had booked a weekend getaway, and I would spend the weekend with Mama Nancy. Mom and Dad left for the airport early on Saturday morning, and were already gone when I woke. From my room, I could smell a mix of frying bacon and coffee. I went downstairs to find Mama Nancy pulling the bacon from the pan.

"Mornin' Lizzy," she said. "Sit down and eat some breakfast. We've got a lot of talking to do today and I'm not about to do it on an empty stomach."

My stomach fluttered with nerves at the thought of finally understanding what happened that day in her room. I sat and ate my breakfast in silence. Mama Nancy nibbled at a piece of bacon while she sipped coffee. When I finished, she took my plate and rinsed it off in the sink. I thought she would make me wait until after the kitchen was cleaned, but she surprised me by leaving the pan on the oven and the dishes in the sink.

"Come along, girl," she said as she walked out of the kitchen.

I hurried after her, my mind whirling with nervous excitement. I was anxious to know what happened that day, but the image of her looking at me with wild-eyed intensity filled me with dread.

We reached her room, and I sat in what had become my chair. Before she sat, she opened her sewing chest and pulled out the family quilt. She carried the quilt to me, laid it across my lap, and then sat in her chair beside me.

"I told you once that this was our family quilt, and that it was very special," she began. "That is all true. What makes it special is another thing entirely. My great grandmother Emily made this quilt when she was a young girl, not much older than you, Lizzy. Emily was a magnificent seamstress, as you can see from the quilt. It's over one hundred and fifty years old and still in beautiful condition."

Mama Nancy sighed and rubbed her temple.

"From here, the story is going to sound like a fairy tale. Lizzy, I'm asking you to keep an open mind. You'll see for yourself one day, but for now, just listen. I'm an old woman, but I've still got all my marbles."

I smiled and nodded.

"When Emily made this quilt, she did something to it. You could say she cast a spell on it, and you wouldn't be far from the truth. The legend says Emily could communicate with the spirits, and the spirits taught her magic. She put that magic into this blanket to protect our family."

I tried to keep the doubt from my face, but Mama Nancy saw it immediately.

"I know, Lizzy. It sounds ridiculous, but I swear it's the truth. When something bad happens to anyone in our family, a tear appears in the quilt. The worse the thing, the bigger the tear. Sometimes, if you're fast enough and good enough with a needle, you can sew it back together before the tear becomes permanent."

I thought back to that day, the tear in the quilt Mama Nancy had been sewing back together. My eyes lit up, and she knew I made the connection.

"You saw it that day when your dad got the test results. You saw the tear in the quilt."

I nodded. "You fixed it," I whispered. "You fixed him."

She nodded back at me and reached over to the quilt in my lap. She unfolded a section and pointed a wrinkled finger at a seam.

"Here," she said.

Sure enough, the seam was so masterfully sewn that it blended in with the rest of the patterns on the quilt. You would never have noticed it without someone showing you.

It all made sense, but was unbelievable.

"Just like that?" I asked. "If something bad happens to me, you can pull out this quilt, sew the tear back together, and I'm fine?"

Mama Nancy frowned and shook her head. "It's not that simple. It doesn't always work. Nature will always take its course. When someone gets old and sick, the quilt won't save them. It doesn't offer immortality. When something unnatural happens, something that wasn't meant to be, that's when we get a chance to fix it. Your father is still a young man. It would've been wrong for him to suffer such a disease. So, I got the chance to fight it. If you're lucky, you may never have to sew the quilt." She paused and exhaled a deep breath. "You may never have to pay the price."

"What price?" I asked.

She looked me in the eye and held my gaze. For a brief second, there was a flicker of the fiery intensity in her eyes. I gasped and leaned back instinctively.

"I'm sorry," she said, lowering her head. Again, she rubbed her temples before looking back up at me. The heat was gone from her eyes.

"The spirits provide the magic, but they don't give it freely."

She reached out and took my hand.

"You'll have to be ready for that," she said.

"Why me?" I asked. "Does Mom know about this? Won't she be the one to take over when you're..." I trailed off. I hadn't realized how much it would hurt to even suggest that Mama Nancy would be gone someday.

"She's not the one. The keeper of the quilt always knows the next in line. My mother wasn't one of us either. My aunt Katherine trained me and handed the quilt down. There's something inside us, something not everyone has." She squeezed my hand. "I saw it on the day you were born. I felt it, like a rope tying us together."

I struggled to take this all in. She was right. It sounded like a fairy tale. I would have written it all off as fantasies of an old woman had I not seen her that day.

"That's enough for now, child," she said. She rose from her chair with a soft grunt. "How about you work on those headbands you were making for your friends? I've got work to do myself."

She shuffled towards the door, and I noticed she was moving slower than usual. She had always been a graceful woman, even in her old age. Now, she moved stiffly, as if every bone in her body ached. As she reached the doorway, I called after her.

"Mama Nancy, you didn't tell me the price," I said. "What is the price we pay the spirits?"

She turned back and gazed at me with tired eyes. "I hope you never have to find out, Lizzy. I hope it with all my heart."

Years passed without further incident. The day in the sewing room and the conversation after faded into a hazy memory that felt more and more like a dream with every passing day. Mama Nancy never mentioned any of it again.

I continued to sew in my free time, and my skill was undeniable. I could not say the same for Mama Nancy. Arthritis had taken hold of her, and her hands were the first to feel the effects. Every day it seemed her hands curled up a little more, the knuckles bulging and swollen. She tried her best to keep up her craft, but it wasn't long before the dexterity loss was too much to overcome. She said it didn't bother her, that she had sewn enough hats and dresses to last a lifetime, but I could see the sadness in her eyes.

I was now sixteen years old and living up the freedom of a newly licensed driver. I spent most of my evenings after school hauling my friends around town. I felt guilty for spending so much time away from home. For the first time in my life, I wasn't spending most of my free time with Mama Nancy. I felt bad for not spending more time with her, but it was difficult to see her in such terrible shape. Her health was deteriorating before our eyes. The lively woman who had practically raised me was nearly gone, and it broke my heart.

It was one of those evenings, out at the mall with my friends, when I received a phone call that changed everything. We were hanging out in the food court when my phone lit up with a picture of my aunt Connie. I didn't talk to Connie regularly, so it was unusual for her to call me.

"Hey Aunt Connie, what's up?" I asked.

"Lizzy, you've got to get to the hospital," she sobbed into the phone. "There was an accident. Your mom and dad were taking Nancy to her doctor's appointment, and, and..." she trailed off.

"And what? What happened?" I nearly screamed into the phone.

"Oh Lizzy, a truck hit them head on."

My stomach rolled, and I clapped a hand over my mouth. My eyes burned with tears. I listened to her sob into the phone for a few seconds before I spoke again.

"Are they alive?" I asked softly, barely recognizing my voice.

"They are, but they're all in bad shape. They had to call Care Flight to take them. It's bad, Lizzy, really bad."

"I'm coming," I said, and without another word, I ended the call.

My friends all stared at me with concerned looks.

"I have to go," I said as I staggered to my feet. "My parents and grandma were in an accident. I have to go."

I didn't wait for their replies. I took off, sprinting through the mall and into the rain-soaked parking lot.

I was halfway to the hospital when I thought of the quilt. The memories flooded over me. What if I could fix this? Without hesitation, I took a hard right and headed away from the hospital. I was going home.

Twenty minutes later, I unlocked the front door of my house and raced up the stairs to the sewing room. I flipped the light switch and immediately knew that wasn't right. The image of Mama Nancy rocking back and forth while the candlelight flickered on her face flashed in my mind. I pulled a box of matches from the top drawer of the nightstand and set to work lighting the candles placed all around the room. I always thought it strange that Mama Nancy kept candles set out around the sewing room that she rarely ever lit. I realized now they were there for when she needed them. Like I needed them now.

Once the candles were lit, I raised the lid of the chest and thrust my hands into the piles of fabrics and yarn. Near the bottom, my fingers sank into the silky texture of the quilt, and I yanked it free. The quilt unfolded in front of me, and I gasped as the gaping tear revealed itself. It was nearly the full width of the quilt.

I sat in my chair, draping the quilt over my lap. I picked up my needle, tied the thread, let my instincts take over, and set to work. The needle bobbed in and out of the quilt, my steady hand driven by years of practice. The only sounds were the soft patter of rain against the windows and the steady creak of the chair rocking back and forth.

As I worked, frustration took hold. I didn't seem to make any progress. Despite every stitch I pulled together, the tear did not appear to be closing. If anything, it was getting longer. What if I was too late? With a renewed sense of urgency, I sewed faster. I sewed faster than I had ever sewn before. A reckless frenzy overtook my care and attention to detail as I desperately worked to close the tear.

I smelled them before I saw them. As I worked, a strange musty scent filled the room. Then I noticed the shadows on the wall. They were bending. Not the flickering sway of the candles. It was more than that. Long, thin forms were moving around the walls. My fingers slowed as I watched them. One by one, they peeled free of the yellow paint and flower printed borders and swooped around the room. I choked back a cry as they dashed about the room, dark apparitions sending the candle flames into a blinding frenzy.

I froze in my chair, no longer rocking, no longer sewing. Though the spirits flashed around the room in chaos, they did so in silence. My trance was broken when I heard the soft ping of a busting stitch. I looked down at the quilt to see my work coming undone, the rip spreading wider again.

I cried out in desperation and returned to stabbing the needle into the quilt. Blood dripped from my fingertips from repeated pokes. I kept my head down and worked, rocking in time with the needle, the specters dancing in my peripheral vision.

I heard a soft whispering all about me, like a swirling wind. I peered up long enough to see that the spirits had formed a circle and were swooping around me. I could barely make out their long, slender forms as they weaved about.

"She sews but does not speak."

"She does not say the words."

"She does not call our names."

The voices came at me from all sides, cold hissing in my ears.

My mind went back to Mama Nancy and that day so long ago. The fire in her eyes. I didn't have to see a mirror to know that the same fire raged in my own. She had been mumbling to herself then. Chanting words I could not make out.

"I don't know the words," I croaked.

The spirits hissed together, sending a piercing pain into my ears.

"Blasphemy!"

"Violator!"

"Corruption!"

"You dare call upon us?"

"One who does not know the words?"

"One who does not know our names?"

The voices rained over me, and I screamed.

"I'm sorry. She never told me the words, didn't tell me your names. Please help me," I begged. "I'll do anything. I'll give anything. Please help me."

"You seek to bring back three from the edge of the abyss. That is no small thing."

"Alas, you are one of the chosen."

"The threads of fate bend to your will."

"If only you say the words."

"If only you speak our names."

"I will say the words! I will say your names! Just tell me what to say," I sobbed.

The spirits slowed until they stood still around me. They were inky black blurs devoid of any features. Too tall and too thin. Three of them formed a triangle around me. In unison, they each reached out a hand, placing one on each of my shoulders and the third on top of my head. My blood ran cold, icy rivers flowing through my veins.

"Do you swear allegiance to the endless, the guardians of forever, the givers of life, the bringers of death?"

"I do, I swear it!"

"Do you willingly offer the price for what you ask?"

"I do."

"Say the words and you shall have your desire."

I stared up at the void where the phantom's face should be.

"SAY THE WORDS!"

I felt the small shred of sanity I had left snap under the weight of its scream. I began to repeat the words. I said them over and over.

"I swear allegiance to the endless, the guardians of forever, the givers of life, the bringers of death. I swear allegiance to the endless, the guardians of forever, the givers of life, the bringers of death."

I felt a hand move from my shoulder, down my arm, and into my own hand. I could feel the emptiness sliding into me as if I were a glove. The fingers of the hand no longer my own picked up the needle and sewed. I watched with a detached sense of being. The thread glowed like white fire as it weaved through the quilt, closing the tear.

No sooner than it began, it was over. The hand slid out of mine and I wailed in agony. The quilt fell from my lap and crumpled to the floor. I could see the damage had been undone. It shimmered in the candlelight, a pristine piece of tailoring.

The spirit in front of me lowered itself until it was inches from my face.

"You must pay the price," it hissed.

I couldn't bring myself to speak, so I only nodded.

The three of them fell upon me, and the sewing room disappeared. I found myself twisting and thrashing through an undulating darkness. The spirits latched on to my skin as if they were sucking the blood from my body. Even in that maddening blackness, I knew what was happening. It wasn't my blood they were stealing. It was time. They were stealing my life away from me. I could feel my youth slipping away, like a light slowly dimming.

I felt like screaming and crying, but I did nothing. I drifted through that void while they took what they wanted. I paid the price.

I woke to a dull thudding sound. I pushed myself up to find I was on the floor of the sewing room. The quilt lay in a rumpled pile beside me. Again, I heard the soft thumping sound. This time, a shout followed it.

"LIZZZY!"

I recognized the voice of my aunt Connie. I pulled my phone from my pocket to see that it was now 12:45am and I had seven missed calls from her.

I climbed shakily to my feet. The world swayed beneath me as I struggled to find balance. I was drained and weak, barely managing the strength to put one foot in front of the other. I finally made it to the front door, flipped the lock, and pulled it open.

I could see the relief wash over her face at the sight of me. She grabbed me by the shoulders and yanked me into her arms.

"What happened to you, girl?" she asked. "You said you were coming and then you never did. I thought something happened to you, too."

"I'm sorry," I said. I paused, trying to come up with a sensible excuse. "I just panicked, and I was upset. I couldn't face it yet, so I came home. I must have fallen asleep."

"I'm so glad you're ok."

"How are they?" I asked. I felt like a fraud. I knew how they were. I had seen to it.

"They're stable, all three of them. It didn't look good at first, but they all came out of it. They're going to make it," she said. She took my hands in hers and squeezed. "They're going to be okay."

I smiled and squeezed back before pulling my hands back to wipe the tears from my eyes. The weight of everything that had happened, everything I had seen, and threatened to break me, but I steeled myself and exhaled deeply.

"Let's go," I said. "I need to see them."

All three of them were in the intensive care unit. Connie stayed in the waiting room while I went back. Mom and Dad were in adjacent rooms. Dad looked bad. Mom looked worse. They both had cuts and deep bruising on their faces. Dad had a broken arm, three broken ribs, and severe lacerations. Mom had a punctured lung and a concussion. They were both going to live, but it would be a long road to recovery.

After spending a few minutes with each of them, I crossed the hall into Mama Nancy's room. Her frail body was battered. She had suffered a broken hip, dislocated shoulder, and a huge gash from her hairline to her jaw. Stitches held her face together and the irony broke me. I collapsed onto my knees and cried. Eventually, the nurse fetched my aunt Connie to take me out of the unit.

Mama Nancy asked for me the next day. She had been in and out of consciousness, but by the afternoon, she had her wits about her. I walked into the room and we locked eyes. She stared back at me with that knowing look I had gotten so used to. Her lip quivered and her eyes welled with tears. I had none left.

"I'm sorry, Lizzy," she whispered. Her voice was cracked and hoarse. "I'm sorry you had to go through that."

"I couldn't lose you guys," I said. "Not when I could stop it."

"If only I could've had more time to prepare you," she sobbed.

I took her hand and kissed her forehead. I knew she meant well, but there was nothing she could have done to prepare me. My mind flashed back to that void. The heat and pressure of the writhing spirits swarming over me. I thought of the innocence and youth I lost. I thought about how someday I would have to pass along the skill and the knowledge to some innocent child. My daughter, my granddaughter, a cousin maybe? Mostly, I thought of the words.

I swear allegiance to the endless, the guardians of forever, the givers of life, the bringers of death. I swear allegiance to the endless, the guardians of forever, the givers of life, the bringers of death. I swear allegiance to the endless, the guardians of forever, the givers of life, the bringers of death.

I AM NOT GONE

The face of the missing child posted on the bulletin board is a mirror. Those are my green eyes, my scraggly blonde hair. It says I was last seen three months ago. I don't understand this. I am not gone.

The news anchor says the search has been called off for the missing local boy. There is video footage of police searching through the woods behind my house. He says I vanished from my backyard in the middle of the afternoon. There are no leads and no evidence to explain my disappearance.

My mother is at home. She doesn't leave anymore. Sometimes I go see her, but I stopped trying to talk to her. She prays that her son will come home. I told her so many times I was home, but she doesn't listen. I screamed at her until my voice gave out, but she still insists I am lost.

My father doesn't live at home anymore. He left after my posters went up around town. He stays with a friend, but mostly I see him at the bar. Sometimes I sit with him, but he doesn't talk to me either. He blames my mother for losing me. He tells people that if she had been watching me, this never would have happened.

My friends at school are sad, but they don't talk about me much anymore. For a while, I still went to class. I sat in my usual seat. I still raised my hand when I knew the answer, but the teacher never called on me. One day she rearranged the desks, and now my seat is gone. I think she didn't want anyone to sit where the missing boy sat.

There is a black tunnel behind me everywhere I go. I hear whispers from within. I am afraid of what might be on the other side. There is something familiar about it I cannot place. I think I have been there before. I think I will go there again. I can feel it reaching for me. The darkness is the only thing that sees me now.

The shadows are alive, and they follow me. I see them from the corner of my eye. I hear them calling my name. They whisper to me when I allow them to get close. They say this world is no longer for me, and I should go with them. I am a memory that has already faded.

I visited my parents to say goodbye. I know they don't hear me, but I may not get another chance. I will go through the tunnel. I must know what is on the other side. I don't know if I can come back. The voices are louder from the edge, and I see movement in the dark. I am afraid, but I will not stop. The shadows take my hand and guide me through the passage. Together, we reach the other side.

Now, I understand.

I am not gone.

THE GIRL ON THE BOARDWALK

Eric was halfway up the hill on The Rocket when he saw the girl on the boardwalk. She wore tight cutoff jean shorts, a navy-blue tank top, and flip-flops. Her dirty blonde hair was shoulder length, with curls that bounced with each step. Eric couldn't take his eyes off her. She walked alone but did not seem to look for anyone. She strolled through the crowds with a casual confidence, suggesting she owned the place. Eric was so hypnotized by her he didn't realize the carts had reached the top until they jerked forward and raced into the drop. He lost sight of her as he plunged down the track.

The Rocket was a big wooden roller coaster that beat the hell out of everyone who dared to ride. It was the only coaster on the boardwalk though, so if you wanted top speed thrills, you rode The Rocket. As the coaster roared through corners and back up smaller hills, Eric scanned the boardwalk for the girl. Each glimpse granted him a brief second to find her, and each time he came up empty.

The carts slammed to a stop, then slowly rolled into the loading station. When the lap bar released, Eric scrambled from the seat and raced out the exit down the winding stone path to the boardwalk. He peered down the strip, looking for any sign of her, but the crowd was thick. From here, she was a needle in a haystack.

"What the hell, man?" shouted a voice from behind him.

Eric turned to find his cousin Noah approaching from the exit line. He shoved a handful of items into Eric's chest.

"All your shit fell out of your pockets. You're lucky I paid attention. What's the deal? Why did you run off like that?"

"Sorry man," Eric replied, putting his phone, wallet, and keys back into his pockets. "I saw a girl."

Noah frowned at him. "Okay, and?"

"I don't know," Eric said. "She was amazing. I have to find her."

"Just like that? You saw a hot girl, so you ditched me to track her down, and then what?"

"I don't know. I just have to find her."

Noah frowned again before letting out a resigned sigh. Eric was the guy that could meet a girl, introduce himself, and leave with her number every time. He was tall and athletic, with a lean muscular frame. His clothes always fit right, and his hair was always perfect. Noah harbored a fair bit of jealousy for his cousin. Eric was who every guy wanted to be. Noah was what most guys were. He wasn't ugly, but he wasn't handsome. He was of average height and a little above average weight. Noah didn't consider himself fat, but the lap bar on The Rocket suggested he might reconsider.

"All right. I know that look, and you won't let this go. Let's find her."

Eric nodded without taking his eyes from the crowd. He would find her, with or without Noah, but he was glad to have his support.

"Come on," Eric said. "She went this way. Blond hair, blue tank top, jean shorts. You'll know her if you see her."

"Yeah, yeah, I got it. The hottest girl on the strip."

"That'll be her."

They moved through the crowd. Eric maneuvered smoothly around and through people. Noah apologized repeatedly as he bumped into people and stepped on toes. The crowd thinned out as they reached the end of the boardwalk. With the rides and food stalls behind them, the view of the ocean dominated the scenery. Noah sucked in a deep breath and did a visual sweep of the area. A few people wandered the pier, watching the sunset over the water, but none matched the description of the girl.

"Maybe she was on a ride or in a shop?"

"Maybe," Eric said.

"Let's go back through again. If we don't see her this time, we can ride something."

"I don't want to ride anything."

"I don't mean for shits and giggles. Bird's-eye view. Get up high and maybe we can find her that way. That's how you found her the first time, right?"

"You're right. Good call. Let's do it."

Together, they made their way back up the boardwalk, this time doing more thorough scans. Eric stopped by the entrance to a souvenir shop and checked the aisles. Noah pushed up to the railing of The Scrambler and watched the faces of riders as the carts whipped towards him, one after another.

They pressed down the strip, one attraction or vendor at a time, scanning lines and seats. Once, Noah thought he found her riding The Spider. Blonde hair and a blue tank top were a match. He didn't think she was really all that. But, as they say, beauty is in the eye of the beholder. He turned and shouted for Eric, who was looking through the line for hand dipped ice cream.

"Eric! Over here!"

Eric raced over and grabbed the railing next to Noah.

"Car number six," Noah said and pointed towards the left side of the ride.

The Spider had four arms coming off the center with four carts on each arm. The arms rotated around the base while the carts rotated freely on the arms, depending on the direction of momentum.

Eric tracked the cart until he got a good look at her. He frowned and shook his head.

"Not even close, dude."

"Damn."

"Keep moving," Eric said.

They were halfway down the strip when Noah put out a hand and stopped Eric.

"We're running out of light. This will be impossible in the dark. I say we hit the swings and try to spot her from up there."

Eric swiveled his head, searching the crowd, the frustration apparent on his face.

"Clock's ticking, bud." Noah pointed over his shoulder toward the ride behind him. "Let's fly."

Eric nodded and hesitantly followed Noah into the line. The Zephyr was like the swing ride you find in kiddie land amusement parks, but on an adult scale. The swings hung from twenty-foot chains. When the operator started the ride, the hydraulic center would raise the swings ten feet into the air, then spin and fan the swings out over the beach and boardwalk. It provided a breathtaking view of the ocean and the strip, especially after dark, when the lights on the boardwalk lit the sky in a fluorescent haze.

The line was short, and they only waited one cycle before they could board. Noah took the first seat he came to after he passed through the entrance. Eric dropped into the seat beside him. He bounced his knee anxiously as he watched the ride attendant check the latches on all the rides before making his way back to the control panel.

At last, the attendant turned the key and pushed the start button. The hydraulics kicked on and the swings slowly rose into the air. The motor hummed to life, and the swings began to twirl.

Noah felt his stomach lurch a little as the swings banked sideways and picked up speed. Roller coasters didn't bother him, but the lack of restraints on the swing made him feel less secure. He knew velocity would keep him in his seat, but that didn't stop his mind from convincing him he was going to fall. He tightened his grip on the chains and glanced at the seat beside him.

Eric looked calm but determined, his eyes flicking back and forth over the crowd. Even in the fiery glow of the boardwalk lights, it was too dark to make out faces. After several spins around, he groaned in frustration. He lost her. Eric looked over at Noah to find him white knuckled and green faced. He would not be of any help.

It was stupid. Eric didn't know why he had been so affected by the girl, but she mesmerized him. Defeated, he resigned himself to the fact that he would not find her.

Then, when he had given up hope, he saw her. His heart leapt in his throat as he caught another glimpse of her as the Zephyr twirled him around. She was right below them, walking the railing around the ride. He watched in two second snippets as she moved around the perimeter. She reached the edge of the pavement and stopped. Her head turned and her eyes fell on the Zephyr and the whirling faces. Eric locked eyes with her and she smiled back in the brief second before the swing forced her from his view.

As he whipped back around, he saw her leave the pavement and walk onto the beach. It made no sense, but Eric knew she wanted him to follow. He felt the hydraulics shift, and the ride slowed. When she came back into view on the next resolution, Eric saw something odd. A new shape that he hadn't noticed before was also on the beach. A large black mass was moving towards the girl. The swings continued to slow and bring Eric closer to the ground. The beach came into view again, and his eyes widened in surprise. A giant man clothed in black was making a direct line for her.

"What the hell?"

"I don't feel so good, man," Noah said. "I think I'm going to be sick."

Eric flashed a quick glance back at Noah.

"I see her. She's on the beach, but there's someone…"

Before Eric could finish his sentence, Noah turned his head away and puked. The crowd erupted in a chorus of shouts.

"I'm sorry," Noah said, just before another wave hit and he vomited again.

The ride slowed to a stop, and Eric scrambled out of his seat.

"I'll be back," he said.

Noah waved him off. "I'm good, man. I'll be fine. Go get her."

Eric bypassed the exit gate packed with riders trying to get away from Noah's mess and hopped over the railing on the beach side of the ride. Right away, he saw the girl. The man was nearly on her, and she seemed oblivious.

"HEY!"

The girl turned and looked back. She smiled and waved at Eric.

"LOOK OUT!" he shouted and pointed toward the man.

She turned just before the man blasted into her. She screamed, but it cut short as the man knocked the wind from her. He picked the girl up over his shoulder and raced off down the beach.

Eric didn't hesitate. He jumped the wooden staircase, closing the gap from the sidewalk to the beach and ran after them. Sand sprayed behind him as he pushed himself as fast as he could go. To his dismay, he did not seem to close the distance between them at all. The large man moved with an unnatural grace and speed, even with the struggling body of the girl kicking and flailing over his shoulder.

To Eric's surprise, the man took a hard left toward the water. Eric watched in confusion as he carried her into the ocean and dove into a wave, disappearing into the dark.

Eric scanned the choppy surface for any sign of them as he approached the water line. He stopped just as the tide washed over his shoes, bent forward with his hands on his knees, and sucked in deep breaths. All the while, he scanned the water. His heart hammered in his chest with a combination of exertion and adrenaline.

At last, he saw her blonde hair emerge from the water. She flailed her arms wildly, and he could just barely hear a faint scream before the wind carried the sound away. Without hesitation, he took off into the water and leaped into an oncoming wave. The water was chilly, but it did not faze him, and he swam further into the vast sea. Like most other athletic endeavors, Eric was an accomplished swimmer, and he moved through the water with a practiced ease.

Again, he saw the girl's arms thrashing about before disappearing into the black depths. He adjusted course and pushed himself harder, his lungs burning as he used every ounce of oxygen his lungs could hold before emerging for air.

Exhausted, he stopped himself. Fear rattled him as he realized he could no longer feel the bottom. He twisted in the water to see he was now approximately fifty yards from the beach. The strip lights were a distant blur, and the roar of the waves replaced all sounds.

He could barely see anything. The water and sky merged into a mosaic of shadows. He considered calling out to the girl, but he knew it was useless. The water lapped around his face as he kicked his feet to stay afloat. Anxiety gripped him as seconds passed with no sign of the girl or her captor. A desperate cry erupted from within him.

Then, a pale arm broke the surface of the water in front of him. It glowed white against the surrounding darkness. Eric knew immediately that it was her, and he frantically grabbed her hand and pulled.

Her face broke the surface of the water, and she exhaled in a massive gasp. Even in the dark, her beauty struck Eric. His heart ached for her, and he pulled her to him.

"I've got you. It's okay, I've got you."

The girl wrapped her arms around him and squeezed tightly.

"No, honey," she replied.

Eric stiffened as he felt her fingernails dig into his back.

"We've got you."

Her nails tore through his shirt and punctured deep into his back, forcing a scream from Eric. He put both hands on her shoulders and tried to push her away. She snarled at him, showing jagged, pointed teeth. Eric pulled his knees up to his chest and kicked. His foot landed cleanly on her chin, snapping her head backwards. The shock of the blow caused her to release her claws from his back, and she dipped under the water.

Eric turned towards the distant lights of the boardwalk and swam, his arms windmilling through the water. He managed only a few yards before he felt a hand clamp on his ankle, yanking him back. He twisted and prepared to fire off another kick, but the vice like grip on his ankle would not break. Another hand grabbed him by the throat before being tossed high into the air. Sailing through the night, he locked eyes with the man below him. He no longer wore the black coat, but there was no mistaking the massive size. The man sneered at him, showing the same shark teeth as the girl. Then water slammed into him like rolling waves of stone. He thrashed about, fighting his way back to the surface. He emerged to see them side by side in front of him. They smiled hideously.

"You see, my love," the girl said. "We've got you."

The man cackled into the night.

Exhausted, Eric watched helplessly as the two leapt at him. The last thing he saw before they dragged him down into oblivion were the scale covered tails where their legs had been.

Noah stared at the bulletin board alongside the pier. He had never noticed how many missing person posters there were, at least not until Eric's picture had joined them. All of them were young men in their teens or twenties.

"Awful lot of runaways," said a voice behind him.

Noah turned to see an older couple had stopped behind him.

The woman shook her head. "What a shame."

Noah nodded to them in reply, then turned and strolled down the strip. He didn't know what happened to Eric, but he knew he wasn't a runaway. Three weeks had passed with no sign of him. The police had done their due diligence and came up empty-handed. Now, Noah followed the only lead he had. Like he'd done every night since, he walked the strip looking for the girl on the boardwalk.

HIGGINS ROAD

"I saw a UFO once."

The guys around the table erupted into raucous laughter, drowning out the already considerable bar racket.

"Of course you fucking did," said Darren. He snatched up his beer bottle and took a long swig. "Was this before or after you saw Bigfoot?"

More laughs assaulted me, and I shook my head.

"Never saw Bigfoot, but I did see a UFO," I replied. I rolled with the ribbing. This was not the first time I had told the story, and it was almost always received in the same dismissive fashion.

Darren gave me a smug smile. He was a sure bet to blow me off. If he couldn't see it or touch it, then it wasn't real. He was a man's man. He could fix your car, help you with many odd jobs, and he was a blast to hang out with and watch football or MMA fights. But throw some philosophical debate or journey into the supernatural at him and he was out.

"I call bullshit," he said.

"Let him tell the story," Mike said from the other side of the table. "I've heard this one before. It's a good one. I don't *believe* it, but it's a good one."

"Come on, man," I exclaimed. "Pete was there. He'll back me up, and he wouldn't bullshit you about it."

"I asked Pete once," Mike said. "He said you guys saw something—I'll admit that—and you're right. Pete isn't the kind of guy that would make shit like that up."

"Thank you," I said.

"I still don't believe you saw a UFO, though," Mike said.

Darren snorted laughter and sipped his beer.

"Fine. Tell your story, Jay. Blow my mind," Darren said. He sat back in his chair, crossed his leg over his knee, and folded his arms across his chest.

"Don't forget the disclaimer," Mike said. "That's the best part."

"Disclaimer?" Darren raised an eyebrow.

I sighed. "We were smoking weed."

Darren choked on his beer, spawning a thunderous coughing fit that drew annoyed looks from the girls at the next table.

"Oh my God, that's perfect," he wheezed, wiping tears from his beet-red face. "Doesn't reduce your credibility at all!"

I rolled my eyes. *Every damned time.*

"Somebody laced that shit," Mike said. "That's my theory."

"It was the same junk weed we always smoked. Never hallucinated on it before that and never have since," I fired back.

"Okay, okay," Darren said, still chuckling. "I want to hear the story. I'm keeping an open mind." He put on a serious face, but that smile still twitched at the corners of his mouth.

"Alright," I began. "So, me and Pete were out on this back road one night. Higgins Road. It's out in the middle of nowhere, off the highway. No houses on it—it just connects two other country roads. It's all flat out there and Higgins is only about a half mile long. At night, you can see headlights coming from either direction. We were both nineteen, both still lived at home. Since we couldn't smoke at home, we cruised the back roads and smoked. Sometimes we'd go out to Higgins and park. If any cars came, which almost never happened, we would jump back in the car and take off. Usually, there were four of us cruising, but that night, it was just me and Pete."

"Convenient," Darren said.

"I wish we had all been there," I replied. "It would be nice to have a little more backup than just Pete. I think it makes him uncomfortable to talk about it."

"I'll give you that," Mike said. "The time I asked him about it, he didn't have much to say. Definitely doesn't have your enthusiasm."

Darren looked at me. His joking demeanor shifted, and a genuine curiosity emerged. "What happened?"

"So, we're out on Higgins. We finished the joint and were just hanging out, smoking cigarettes and bullshitting. Clear night, no clouds. Off in the distance, we see what we think is a plane flying towards us. Nothing to get excited about. It flies over and we don't think anything of it. Couple minutes later, another plane comes from the same direction. This one flies over just like the first. Then another plane. At this point, we know something weird is going on. It's not normal for three planes to be flying in the same direction that close together."

I took a drink of my beer. Darren eyed me from across the table. He was not impressed.

"At this point, we're not doing anything except watching the sky," I continued. "Then, coming over the horizon, there are way more planes coming. I didn't count, but I would guess maybe ten or fifteen. They're all flying in the same direction. I gave Pete an "are you seeing this shit?" look. I look back to the sky and all these lights are flying over us. Then, out of nowhere, one drops down on top of us. I'm talking low and slow. It couldn't have been more than a hundred feet up. I could see details on the bottom of it—it was black with panels and tubing running across it. It was huge. I mean, it blocked out the sky while it was over us. It reminded me of that movie with Will Smith and Jeff Goldlbum."

"*Independence Day,*" Mike suggested.

"Yeah, that one. The craziest part was that it didn't make any fucking noise. No motor sounds, no humming or buzzing. Nothing."

I paused and watched Darren for his reaction. His eyebrow was raised.

"Then what?" he asked.

"I think it stopped. I can see it in my mind like it happened yesterday. The ship is in the air above us. It's like my brain took a still frame photograph."

"Did you get beamed up?" Darren asked. He smiled, but the question didn't sound like a joke.

"I don't think so," I replied. "It's weird, but the next thing I can remember, the ship was gone, and all the lights were off in the distance. We could still see at least a dozen lights moving away. We jumped in the car and tried to follow them, but obviously that didn't work."

I finished my beer in two big swallows, clanked the bottle down on the table, and waited to see what Darren would say.

"That's it?" he asked.

"Yeah, that's it."

Mike looked back and forth between us with an amused smile.

"Yeah," Darren said after a long pause. "I believe you."

"Really?" I asked. The surprise on my face must have been blatant.

"I believe you saw *something*," he said. "But I think it was a military operation—some kind of test flight or something."

I frowned. "No way."

"Why not? You were high as a kite and a nineteen-year-old kid. Of course, you would think it was a UFO. I probably would have too if I'd been there. If you look at it through the lens of adulthood, it was the military. I guarantee it. Think about it, the air force base is fifty miles from here. Who knows what kind of crazy tech they've got over there?"

"I get what you're saying, but that wasn't it. If you had seen it, you would understand."

"I'm with Darren," Mike chimed in. "It's a great story, man, but if you take off the weed influenced glasses of your youth, you'll see it's a hell of a stretch."

I sighed and finished off my beer. "Agree to disagree."

Mike and Darren snorted laughter.

"I gotta hit the head," I said. I swayed as I stood, buzzing from the alcohol. I pushed the chair in and worked my way through the bar. The Saturday evening crowd was piling in and nearly all the tables were taken. I turned the corner down the back hallway toward the restrooms. A few girls formed a short line outside the women's room, but the men's room was mercifully vacant. A heavy urine smell assaulted my senses. I sneered in disgust but pressed on to the urinal.

As I relieved myself, a soft *ding* sounded from my pocket. With my free hand, I pulled out my phone, and the screen came to life with a text from Pete.

What a coincidence, I thought. I hadn't spoken to Pete in several weeks, and I get a text out of the blue minutes after I told our story. Curious, I swiped up on the screen, letting the facial recognition unlock it, and opened the text.

What did you do?

I frowned at the phone. I situated myself and zipped my jeans, then laid the phone down on top of the hand dryer, washed up, hit the dryer for a few seconds, and returned to the text.

What do you mean?

A text bubble appeared with rotating dots to indicate that Pete was typing. I stared at the bubbles as they shifted back and forth, my slight buzz making the animation seem a little more elaborate than it really was. After a moment, the phone dinged again.

They're outside. They came back again. I haven't told anyone. I swear. What did you do?

My forehead wrinkled as I tried to make sense of what Pete was saying.

I don't understand. Who came back? What are you talking about?

Instantly, the text bubbles appeared again.

Stop talking about them.

They're coming for you.

I stared at the last text. *Who's coming?* A feeling of unease slipped over me, and suddenly the restroom seemed very small. I started to reply when another text message alert appeared, this time from Darren.

You get your dick stuck in there or what? LOL

I chuckled and felt the tension release in my shoulders. Darren's text was a welcome diversion from the unsettling conversation with Pete. I dropped the phone back into my pocket and stepped back out into the hallway. Immediately, I knew something was wrong.

The bar was silent. The chorus of shouts and laughter that followed me into the restroom were gone. Even the televisions mounted on the walls were muted. The hall was empty. The line of girls I'd seen upon entering the restroom was gone. Cautiously, I walked down the hall back towards the bar proper. My footfalls echoed loudly in the silence. My heartbeat increased steadily as my internal warning signs began to fire. I reached the end of the hall and stepped around the corner.

Four figures stood alone in the bar. I gasped as my mind scrambled to make sense of the scene. The figures were humanoid in shape, but the similarities ended there. They were featureless and solid white. They pulsed with energy. Their glowing white forms made my eyes water, forcing me to cast my eyes to the floor. Looking at them felt like staring at the sun. The air buzzed with energy. I could hear a faint static crackling sound, and the hair stood on my arms.

"There is an error in your programming," said a voice.

Confused, I looked back at the figures, squinting against the light. Each word the figure spoke carried a different pitch and tone.

"You have been instructed on previous occasions to speak nothing of your encounter."

The words skipped at random between both male and female voices. Some of them even sounded familiar.

"Your companion does not exhibit the same malfunction."

The voice seemed to emanate from all of them simultaneously.

"Can you explain this deviation to protocol?"

I flinched at the word protocol. That was my father's voice. Placing his voice opened a floodgate. I knew all the voices. These were voices from my past. Old friends, ex-girlfriends, and family, all cut up and reassembled like a ransom note. They were pulling fragments from my memories, somehow linking to my mind. Whatever these beings were, they couldn't communicate with me naturally.

"I don't understand." My voice was weak, and the words trembled.

The glowing figures turned toward each other, then turned back to me. They did not speak, but I sensed an understanding passing between them.

"Reprogramming required once more. Implant required. Failure may result in project termination."

The figures moved toward me in unison, drifting seamlessly through the bar tables, touching nothing along the way. Through the fog of crippling fear, a thought occurred to me. If these things were pulling from my mind, maybe I could use that to my advantage. I gathered every bit of mental clarity I could muster and screamed in my thoughts. The beings staggered and slowed. Their glowing forms flickered with vibrations from the mental blast. Seizing the moment, I turned and made a dash for the exit. I only made it a few feet before my thoughts of escape were dashed out, and they surrounded me. Two of them grabbed me by the arms, pinning them down. Low voltage electricity rippled across my skin. Another moved behind me, wrapped one arm across my chest, and the other across my forehead. I struggled to free myself but could not break loose. The last of them reached its glowing hand up to my chin. A desperate moan escaped me as tendrils unfurled from the tip of its fingers, clamping onto the underside of my chin. I hissed, and my muscles seized as the appendages pierced my skin and invaded my body. Pain erupted in my head as they snaked up through my mouth, into the nasal cavity, and into my skull. They scattered and spread to different points inside my head. Their pointed tips sank into the soft brain tissue, and my vision exploded into blinding white light. Images scrolled past at incredible speed. Memories of my childhood roared past; recess on the playground in elementary school, little league baseball games, holding hands with Lindsey Powers in 8th grade, high school football, graduation, partying—then, the picture show stopped, and Pete and I stood on Higgins Road.

Once again, I stared up at the aircraft in the sky. This was where my memories of that night ended. A crackling sound filled the air and a blinding light appeared on the underside of the craft, cloaking us in a dull yellow glow. The light intensified and erupted in a violent flash.

We were no longer on Higgins Road. Pete and I were strapped to metal tables in a narrow room with low ceilings. I pushed against the restraints, but they held firm. The glowing white figures from the bar surrounded us. One of them inserted a tube down my throat. I gagged and choked as my throat restricted, fighting against the invasion. My breath came in frantic bursts through my nose while I fought the bile rising in my throat. Pete gasped and moaned. I couldn't see him, but he was nearby, undoubtedly suffering through the same torment as me.

Another of the creatures held the end of the tube. I watched in wide-eyed terror as a tendril of glowing light separated from his fingertip and wriggled into the tube. It slithered through and disappeared into my mouth. I tried to scream, bucking against the restraints, but the cold metal straps held firm. Something wormlike moved in my stomach. Heat engulfed me from the inside out. The thing squirmed around inside me, from one body part to the next. Agony gripped me. It slithered up my spine and came to a stop at the base of my skull. There was a moment of intense pressure, and I blacked out.

When I came to, Pete and I stood on Higgins Road watching the lights drift away. I remember now. We are programmed to forget. Instructed to be silent. We are carriers of them.

"Where the hell is he?"

Darren scanned the crowded bar, but there was still no sign of Jay.

"It's been like twenty minutes," Mike said. "Must be taking a shit."

"Shit or get off the pot, man," Darren said, pushing away from the table. "We've got to go. Leslie's party started an hour ago."

The two of them pushed through the crowd. They rounded the corner into the back hallway to see the line for the men's room was five guys deep. A burly man in a Slayer tee shirt at the front of the line pounded on the door.

"Hurry the fuck up!" he shouted.

Darren and Mike looked at each other, unsure if they should laugh or be concerned. Mike pushed past the line and approached Slayer-guy.

"Hey man, our friend's in there. Has been for a while."

"Fuck yeah, it's been a while," the guy said. "I'm about to kick the door in."

"Easy, big guy," Darren said. "Let us check on him."

He grabbed the knob and twisted, but the door was locked.

"You think I'd still be standing here if it wasn't locked, dickhead?"

Darren shot the drunk man an annoyed look, but didn't retaliate. Instead, he twisted the knob and forced his shoulder against the wood. The lock was cheap, and the door banged open.

Jay stood motionless in the middle of the room, back to the door, undisturbed by the noise. Darren and Mike closed in around him. Mike put a hand on his shoulder and turned him gently.

"You okay, buddy?"

Jay stared blankly, and then his eyes came to life. He blinked and exhaled deeply, as if he had been holding his breath.

"What?" Jay asked. "What happened?"

"You tell us," Darren said. "You've been in here forever. That dude out there is ready to beat your ass—right after he takes a piss."

"You okay?" Mike asked. "You looked pretty out of it for a second."

"Yeah," Jay said. "I'm good."

"You sure?" Darren smiled slyly. "The aliens didn't come and abduct you again, did they?"

Jay turned quickly to Darren and smiled. "Nah, no aliens. You're probably right about it being a military test flight or something. I just tell the story to get people going."

Mike looked questioningly at Jay,chuckled, but let it go. Something seemed off, but he was too buzzed to figure it out.

"Let's get out of here. Leslie's party and all those fine ladies await," Darren exclaimed. He led the way out of the restroom. "Enjoy your piss, big man," he called out as they passed by Slayer-guy.

"Fuck you," the big drunk called back.

Darren chuckled, and the trio stepped out into the warm summer night. Jay turned his eyes to the clear sky. A glowing orb streaked across. There was a tickle at the back of his neck, and he nodded.

Reprogramming complete.

OF BEING A PALLBEARER

I wrote off the first thump as a car door closing in the distance. There were dozens of them lined up the narrow roads sectioning off the cemetery. The crowd of people around the tent was sizable, but there were likely stragglers still making their way to join the service. I thought nothing else of it, adjusted my grip on the cold casket handle, and continued the slow march toward the gravesite.

A low rumble of thunder threatened a coming storm, and a scan of the dark clouds building on the horizon suggested agreement. The second thump, though nearly lost in the thunder, caught my attention. I turned my head to the right and looked at my cousin Bill, my eyebrow raised quizzically. He did not notice. I could see the red-rimmed glaze of his eyes and knew his thoughts were with our lost grandfather.

I did not share the same sadness. I hadn't seen my grandfather in nearly ten years. Prior to that, our relationship was civil. Even as a child, my grandfather had never shown much interest or affection toward me. I harbored a fair bit of jealousy against my cousins. I was always included in group activities, but I always felt like a third wheel. To this day, I don't know why he treated me differently. I'm sure he loved me, but let's just say if he had to choose a favorite grandchild, I wouldn't make the finals. That I had been asked to be a pallbearer at his funeral was a result of numbers. They needed a sixth man, and I was the last grandchild left undrafted. Of course, I accepted the invitation as an honor. It was the polite thing to do.

As we crossed the pavement and stepped into the soft grass near the gravesite, a third thump rattled the casket. I felt a subtle vibration in the handle. Startled, I cleared my throat and looked at the collection of cousins around me. From behind, my oldest cousin Frank put a hand on my shoulder.

"You okay, Teddy?"

"Did you hear that?" I whispered.

"Hear what?"

"That thump."

I craned my neck around to look at him. Our cousin Ben eyed me suspiciously from the opposite back corner of the casket.

"I didn't hear anything," Frank replied.

I almost told him I thought it came from the casket, but Ben's hard gaze changed my mind. Something in his look told me to keep my mouth shut.

"Never mind," I said.

We reached the graveside and sat the casket down. My mother Alice and my uncles Tom and Danny were seated in folding chairs lined up in front of the grave. I took my position behind my mother and placed a comforting hand on her shoulder. She reached up and squeezed it in return.

Much like myself, she did not have a close relationship with her father. There was no family drama to create a divide. They simply weren't close. Maybe it was partly because of how little interest he had shown in me as a child. Maybe not. We never talked about it. His passing saddened her, as was natural. She was not, however, broken by it.

With everyone having taken their place, the pastor began his routine. Everyone bowed their heads in prayer as he asked God to comfort us in our time of grief. I raised my head slightly and looked around me. Off to the side of the gathering, I saw Ben standing by himself. Like me, his head was not bowed in prayer. Instead, he gazed at me. Our eyes locked, and he raised a single finger to his mouth, signaling me to be quiet. I tilted my head in confusion. Ben lowered the finger and nodded slightly toward the coffin. As if on cue, the loudest thump yet rattled the coffin. The arrangement of flowers on top shifted, and a single petal from a pink rose floated slowly down into the grave and out of sight.

Ben quickly raised the finger to his lips again. To my surprise, the pastor droned on with his prayer and none of the other mourners seemed to have heard the thump at all. I looked back at Ben. Both his hands were raised as he signaled for me to stay calm.

Reluctantly, I turned my attention back to the service. I waited for another thump to sound from within the coffin, but to my relief, it remained silent. The pastor gave a brief message, reading a few verses from a battered Bible, closed with another prayer, and concluded the service. As the crowd dispersed, Ben came up behind me and whispered in my ear.

"Come to my place tonight."

"You heard that shit, right?" I asked.

"Come to my place," he repeated. "We'll talk then."

Before I could respond, he took off across the cemetery at a brisk walk. I watched him climb into his rusted out pickup truck and pull away. My mother gave me a nod to suggest that she was ready to leave. I nodded back, but before I followed her to the car, I stepped towards the graveside and placed my hand on the coffin. I nearly knocked on the lid, but then stopped. I was sure that if I did, my grandfather would knock back.

I pulled up to the curb in front of Ben's apartment at quarter to nine. The storm that threatened the funeral service had fulfilled its promise, and a steady rain had fallen all evening. I climbed from the car and jogged up the sidewalk to Ben's door. Years ago, this was a path I took at least once a week. Ben was less than a year younger than me, and we grew up together. We spent many Friday nights playing Xbox or watching movies with a case of beer dwindling between us. Eventually, life did what it does and pushed us in separate directions. No hard feelings or falling out, it just happened.

Knocking on the door filled me with a sad nostalgia for the good times. In my head, I could see Ben opening the door with the half smile he always wore back then, a can of beer in one hand and a fresh one for me in the other.

The Ben that opened the door did not have the youthful enthusiasm I remembered, but he still wore the half smile I remembered so fondly.

"Come on in, Teddy."

"No Halo and Coors Light?" I joked.

Ben chuckled and slapped me on the shoulder.

"Not tonight, man."

I pulled off my damp jacket, hung it on the coat rack by the door, and dropped onto the couch. The living room had changed little in the years since I'd been here last. The tv was bigger; the Xbox was now a One instead of a 360, but otherwise it felt the same.

Ben sat opposite me in a worn-out recliner. An awkward silence fell over us, and I bounced my knee in response to my nerves. I felt ridiculous saying what I was thinking, but Ben didn't seem to be in a hurry to jump into it either. Finally, I exhaled a deep breath and took the plunge.

"Our dead granddad was knocking on the inside of his coffin while we carried it to his grave. Judging by the lack of panic and hysteria, no one but us heard it. That about sums it up, right?"

Ben smiled and nodded. The bizarre nature of my statement was not lost on him.

"Pretty fucking wild, isn't it?"

"Pretty fucking wild doesn't cover it, Ben! What the fuck is happening here, man? That could not have happened. And you, you acted like it wasn't a surprise. Is this some kind of elaborate prank?"

"You're not being punked," he replied. He looked amused as he watched me struggle with the lunacy of our discussion.

"I don't think this is funny."

"I know," Ben said. "I'm sorry. I'm just glad it was you that heard the call. I hoped it would be you."

"Heard the call? What are you talking about? Come clean or I'm out, man. I'm about to lose my shit."

Ben got to his feet and motioned for me to follow. He grabbed my jacket and tossed it to me.

"Fair enough," he said. "I'll explain on the way."

"The way to where?" I asked.

"The cemetery. We have to dig him up."

I followed Ben to his truck in a daze. The whole thing felt like a fever dream. I pulled open the passenger door and saw two shovels in the truck bed, along with a battery-powered lantern tossed haphazardly behind the seat.

"We're really fucking doing this, aren't we?"

"We better. I mean, he's not going to suffocate or anything, but he'll be good and pissed off if we leave him down there much longer."

I turned and looked at Ben as he pulled the truck onto the road. The passing streetlights illuminated his face in pulses, and I could see the shine of excitement in his eyes.

"What is he?" I asked.

Ben cocked his head at me.

"Grandpa. How is he alive down there? What is he?"

"That part, I think I have to let him tell you," Ben answered. "What I can say is that we were chosen. Grandad brought me into the fold a couple of years ago. Right about the time you started doing your own thing. That's kinda why I didn't try harder to stay in touch."

Ben looked at me, and for the first time, his smile faltered. "I'm sorry about that, truly."

Unexpectedly, I had to fight a lump in my throat and my eyes stung with the threat of tears. I hadn't realized until that moment how much I missed Ben these last few years.

Ben sensed my reaction and backhanded my knee playfully. "It's all good now, brother. We've got all the time in the world."

I collected myself and continued.

"What do you mean, he brought you into the fold?"

"I mean, he told me the secrets. Showed me who he really is," Ben said. He took his eyes off the road for a moment to look at me. "He showed me who I really am."

"And who are you, really, then?" I asked.

"Who are we? That's the question you should ask, Teddy. Who are we? You're in this now. You heard the call. He told me how it would go, right before he died, or whatever you want to call it. You know what I mean."

"No, I don't know what you mean, Ben," I fired back.

"He told me I was his left hand, and he would call for his right when the time came. The chosen would hear the call. And it was you. I'm so glad it was you."

We rode the rest of the way to the cemetery in silence. I didn't really have any answers to my questions, but I got the feeling that Ben would not elaborate on much of anything beyond us being "chosen".

Ben checked the rearview mirror to make sure there were no head-lights coming up behind us before turning onto the short lane to the cemetery gate. He killed our headlights, and the car plunged into dark-ness as we entered. The rain had tapered off, but the cloud cover blocked nearly all the moonlight. Despite the lack of headlights, Ben maneuvered through the cemetery with a practiced ease. He stopped the truck next to a large tree fifty yards from Grandpa's grave.

Together, we climbed out of the truck. Without instruction, I grabbed the lantern from behind the seat. I turned it over in my hands, trying to find the power switch. Before I could, Ben whistled sharply.

"Not yet," he whispered. "Only if we need it."

I nodded and lowered the lantern to my side. Ben grabbed the shovels from the bed of the truck, and we marched through the shadows. I don't know that I could have found my way in the dark, but Ben seemed to know exactly where he was going. I got the feeling this was not the first time he had made this trip in the dark.

The loose dirt from the grave came into view. Mounds of flowers and baskets lie around the headstone Grandpa bought years ago. The stone was black granite. The top was cut in such a way that it looked like rolling waves. I read the inscription.

Matthew Von Erich

March 11, 1957 -

He lived life as if his days would never end.

"Pretty on the nose, isn't it?" Ben asked, chuckling softly.

In answer, a muffled thump sounded from within the soil. I jerked and took a couple of steps back. My heart pounded and my face flushed.

Ben turned and tossed a shovel at me.

"Let's get to it, Teddy. He wants out."

Thirty minutes later, my shovel hit the lid of Grandpa's coffin. Ben looked at me and nodded. Though the night air was cool, we were both drenched in sweat. Specks of dirt covered us from head to toe. My back and shoulders ached, and I felt blisters rising on my hands.

Ben dropped to his knees and swept the last bit of dirt away. Slowly, the bronze color of the coffin lid appeared. Ben pulled a metal key from his pocket.

"Where'd you get that?" I asked.

"Grandpa gave it to me. It's the sealing key. It opens the casket."

I nodded as if this made complete sense, and we hadn't just dug up our grandfather's grave.

"Step back," Ben ordered.

I moved behind him to the foot of the coffin. He reached down into the dirt and worked the key until the casket lid released. He turned back and smiled.

"Here we go, Teddy."

Ben pulled the lid open and stepped back beside me. Our grandfather stared up at us.

The visitation and memorial service had been closed coffin, so I had not seen my grandfather prior to the burial. In fact, I had not actually seen my grandfather in nearly ten years. I had prepared myself to see a withered version of the man I remembered. Instead, I saw exactly the man I remembered. A decade had passed and yet the telltale marks of aging had not touched him. His black hair had not thinned, nor were any traces of gray to be found. His face was tight and full of color, with no wrinkles of any kind. He looked first at Ben and then at me. The corner of his mouth pulled up into a slight smile.

"Theodore," he said softly.

The sound of his voice was the final straw. I gasped and collapsed backwards into the jagged wall of dirt behind me. My mind collapsed under the strain of every bizarre moment of the past eight hours. Ben reached out to steady me, but I thrashed against his advance.

"Stay away," I snarled. My heart pounded in my chest, and my lungs burned. I was gasping in shallow bursts. Spots of white filled my vision.

"I think he's having a panic attack, Pap," Ben said.

The world swayed in front of me. In the distance I heard a soft rustling, and then I felt a warm hand against my forehead. My sight cleared long enough for me to see my grandfather crouched in front of me.

"Sleep," he whispered.

Darkness took me.

I woke up and found myself in a bed. I had been stripped down to my boxers. I sat up and struggled to focus my eyes on the room around me. As my mind cleared, familiar posters on the wall sparked recognition. This was Ben's bedroom.

I scrambled out of the bed, jerking the blankets onto the floor as I stood. I scanned the room but did not see my clothes. A basket of unfolded laundry sat next to the door, so I rummaged through until I found a pair of basketball shorts and a t-shirt. Dressed, I pulled open the bedroom door and walked down the short hallway into the living room.

Ben and our grandfather sat on the couch waiting for me. Grandpa still wore the suit he had been buried in. Ben had showered and now wore fresh jeans and a hoodie. I stared back at the two of them with a mixture of emotions. Part of me was in awestruck fascination at the situation. Another part of me threatened another panic attack and the urge to run for the door and never look back.

"Sit down, Theodore," said my grandfather. He held out a hand and motioned to the chair across from them.

"How did I get here?" I asked.

"We carried you back to the truck," said Ben. "Well, first me and Pap filled the grave back in, then we carried you to the truck."

"Benjamin, please," said Grandpa. "I have asked you repeatedly to stop calling me Pap. Our relation to one another is deeper than the traditional naming. I am no longer your grandfather. You are no longer my grandsons. We are brothers for all time. I am Matthew. You are Benjamin and Theodore."

Ben looked at me and rolled his eyes. "All right, Matthew. I think you should explain to Theodore what's happening before he freaks out again."

I nodded in agreement. "I'm sitting in my cousin's apartment with our dead grandfather we dug up because he's not dead, and now he's instructing me to call him Matthew. I'm kind of freaking the fuck out here, guys. What is happening? Is this some kind of mental break delusion? Am I even really here?"

"You are here," replied Matthew. "You will find my history to be quite incredible, but I dare say that after all you have seen today, you will believe it. My gravestone says I was born in 1957. That is not the case. I adopted this existence in 1957. My true birth date is unknown even to me. I have walked this earth for millennia. I saw the gardens of Babylon. I felt the desert sands between my toes as the pyramids of Giza were constructed. I have seen the rise and fall of one civilization after another. I have crossed the seas and lived lifetimes all over the world. Alas, my curse is I have done this alone. Time after time, lives beyond memory, I have watched those I love grow old and die. My torment is I must withstand that sorrow without end. I do not age, and I do not die."

"What are you?" I asked.

"There is no name for it. I am not a vampire, living in darkness and feasting off human blood. I am not a monster. To answer your questions truthfully, I don't know what I am. I have no memory of being a child. I have always been as you see me. I know no master, no creator. I know no purpose. I move from place to place, life to life, blending into the world as best I can. I have studied texts from history lost and forgotten. There are primal energies that flow through all of creation. Magic is as good a word as any. I sense my existence is tied to that magic. I have made it my life's mission to understand it. Perhaps then I will understand myself. I do not believe I exist for no reason."

He paused and took a sip from a glass of water. He stared at me, and I knew he was judging how much of this I believed. Despite everything, the answer was all of it. I believed every word. As if he read my mind, he nodded.

"That brings me to you and Benjamin. I have studied ancient texts, and I have learned much of the possibilities. The repeated sadness of building families to see them pass on to the next existence when I cannot follow became too much for me to take. Through my studies, I discovered a possibility for me to gain companions. It has taken hundreds of years to compile the required pieces, but I have finally succeeded. I won't explain the process to you, as you will not understand. The result is I can share my seemingly endless existence with two. One by choice, and one by connection. After considering all my living relations, I chose Benjamin to join me."

He placed a hand on Ben's knee and patted softly.

"I felt he could withstand the mental burden that such a thing carries. He also makes me laugh," Matthew said with a smile.

Ben chuckled and rolled his eyes again, but I could see the pride he felt in being chosen.

"You, Theodore, you heard the call. You are the connection. The primal magic that binds the world and fuels my existence is alive in you as well. When the time came for me to leave this chapter of my life, you were the one who heard the call. I knocked at the door of eternity, and you answered."

He stood, crossed the room, and picked up a brown leather bag I hadn't noticed previously. From within, he pulled an ornate metal flask and two small cups not much larger than shot glasses.

"Now you must make a choice. I have told you only a small bit of my story and of what is coming. I would never force this on either of you. You must choose. This flask holds the nectar of my being. It contains many ingredients in precise amounts. If you drink from this flask, you will ignite the fibers of the magic that burn in me, and it will burn in you. Together, the three of us will carry on into the future until the end."

Matthew removed the cap from the flask and poured an amber colored clear liquid into the cups and handed one to each of us.

"Will you join me on this journey, Benjamin and Theodore, my left and right hands, my companions."

I looked at Ben. The cup in his hand was shaking slightly from the excitement coursing through him. He nodded enthusiastically. I glanced once more at my grandfather. He stood with his arms crossed and I could see the optimism and hope in his face. I looked back at Ben and nodded. Together, we threw back the cups and swallowed the amber liquid.

I closed my eyes as heat crawled through my veins. My brain felt as if every nerve ending was on fire. Faintly, I felt the cup slip from my fingers and distantly bounce off the floor. After that, the world became white fire, and I knew nothing at all.

I can see the island in the distance, just breaking over the horizon. The boat sways gently on the waves. Seagulls swoop around the boat, confirming we are finally close to land. I don't know how long we've been at sea, because frankly, time means nothing anymore. Ben and Matthew stand beside me. We remained back home only long enough to make arrangements explaining our absence. Ben and I had gone on vacation together and then gone missing. That was the hardest part. I thought often of my mother, and the pain she must be going through. I'd like to reach out to her and let her know I am ok, but that may never happen. Too many questions I can't answer.

I don't know where we are going or what we will do when we get there. I only know we will help Matthew continue to find his way, and hopefully find out what he is and the purpose of all this. Not just what he is, but what we are. We are in this together now. And so, we carry on wherever the winds take us. We live our days as if our days will never end.

SHE'S ALWAYS BEEN MINE

Vic watched the reunion through the large front window of the diner. His knee bounced rapidly, and a white-knuckled fist tested the integrity of the coffee cup in his hand.

"Fucking asshole," he muttered.

"You say something, Vic?"

Startled, Vic turned to see Dotty standing just on the other side of the counter, holding a coffee pot in one hand and a plate of biscuits and gravy in the other. A splash of grease had stained the already dingy apron she wore over her baby blue dress.

"No, just talking to myself," he replied before turning back to the window.

She followed his gaze out onto the street. "Well, would you look at that! I do believe that's Aaron Peterson. Mitch told me he might come in for the holidays."

Vic gritted his teeth. "Yeah, looks like it."

Dotty leaned across the counter toward him and nudged his arm with her elbow. "Looks like Shelly sure is happy to see him." She chuckled and gave Vic a mischievous wink. She topped off his coffee and then moved on down the counter to deliver the breakfast plate.

Vic briefly considered throwing the cup of steaming coffee at the back of her head and then using the shattered glass to tear open her throat. He smiled at the thought, then took a sip from the cup instead.

He turned his attention back to Aaron and Shelly, who were now sharing an awkward embrace on the sidewalk. Shelly wore a long brown coat with a pink scarf wrapped around her neck. Her long brown curls were pulled up under a knit hat. She looked gorgeous, same as she always did.

As much as he hated to admit it, Aaron looked great as well. He was dressed in business casual, every stitch tailored to his lean physique. His black hair was combed neatly, and black stubble outlined a powerful jaw. He smiled at Shelly as she spoke, and even from a distance Vic could see the dazzling white, perfect teeth.

For fuck's sake, Vic thought. *Looks like he just walked off a fucking magazine cover.*

The two finished pleasantries, and Shelly walked away down the sidewalk, disappearing from Vic's view in the diner. He stared at Aaron, who watched Shelly go with a thoughtful gaze.

Keep looking, you piece of shit. I'll give you something to look at, mother fucker. He felt his elbow jitter as his biceps tensed. He grabbed the top of the coffee cup and slammed it sharply against the counter. The glass erupted and hot coffee sprayed against his palm.

Several startled patrons turned toward him, and Dotty rushed over.

"Good heavens, Vic! What happened?"

Vic hissed as he turned his hand over. A jagged cut ran across the meat of his palm, and angry blisters were already forming.

"It's okay, Dotty. I just dropped the cup and tried to grab it. Stupid of me."

Dotty eyed the gash on his palm warily. "You should go see Mitch. That looks like it might need stitches."

"No, I'll be fine," Vic said. "No need for Doc Peterson. I'll just go clean it up and wrap it in some gauze if you've got any."

Dotty disappeared into the kitchen, then returned with a first aid kit. She handed Vic a few gauze pads and a roll of medical tape. "I don't know Vic. That looks pretty deep."

"Not my first cut, Dotty," he said and then gave his best effort at a laugh. "Don't worry about it. Sorry for the mess. Let me wrap this up and then I'll clean it for you."

"You'll do no such thing. Go take care of that."

Vic nodded and took his supplies to the small restroom in the back of the diner. He ran cold water over his hand, wincing. As he watched the blood run in diluted trails into the sink, he imagined it coming from Aaron's face. He could see that perfect smile bashed to pieces as he hammered fist after fist until only a ruined mess remained. *You can't have her. She's mine. She's always been mine.*

He dried his hand quickly with paper towels and then wrapped it up in several layers of gauze before the blood could escape. He checked himself in the mirror before leaving. His flannel shirt was worn but clean, and his bright blue eyes did not convey the intense rage he felt inside. On the surface, he was a handsome young man. Most girls in town had told him so, but he had no interest. Those girls weren't Shelly.

Satisfied, he left the restroom and headed to his stool to grab his jacket.

"Vic Derringer, is that you?"

Vic stopped mid-step and cringed. He recognized the voice, and his blood boiled. He turned slowly to find Aaron sitting in the booth just outside the restroom.

"Aaron, how you doin'?" He kept his voice neutral, trying to keep his disdain from showing through.

Aaron slid from the booth and stuck out a hand. Vic shook it with slightly more force than he intended.

"So good to see you, man!" Aaron flashed a glowing smile. "You look good. How've you been?"

"I'm good. On my way out. Working for Deke out on the docks."

"That's great. Sometimes I wish I would've stuck around. I miss this place. I'm in the city now, but this is still home, you know?"

"Yeah. Well, listen, I have to get going."

"Sure, man," Aaron said. He laughed and grabbed Vic's hand again, this time pulling him into a half hug. "God, it's good to see you. First, I run into Shelly, and now you."

Victor stiffened at the mention of Shelly and stepped away.

"She looks amazing. Kicking myself for letting her get away. We're planning to meet up tonight. Wouldn't that be something, huh? Old flames reignited."

Vic felt blood rushing to his face. He felt the cold weight of his pocketknife against his thigh. It would only take a second, maybe two, to pull the knife from his jeans, flip the blade open, and drive the point right up the underside of Aaron's jaw, buried to the hilt. The dipshit wouldn't even see it coming.

Instead, he nodded. "That would be something. I really have to go, but I'm sure I'll see you around."

"Great, I'll see you. Maybe we can get together and have a few beers later?"

"Sure," Vic replied. He was already moving toward his stool to retrieve his jacket. "We'll have to do that."

Without looking back, Vic slipped on his jacket and left the diner. The brisk December air welcomed him onto the sidewalk. He inhaled deeply; the breeze felt like icy hands on his flushed face. Rather than heading south down Decatur Street toward the dock, he went north. Deke would have to handle the dock on his own today. There were more pressing matters at hand.

Two blocks down from the diner, Vic stopped and peered into a small boutique. Shelly was at the counter, where he knew she would be. The shop was empty, and he considered going in and talking to her, telling her she needed to stay away from Aaron. He was trouble and only going to cause her grief. She needed to understand that no one was going to love her like he did. No one.

Shelly looked up from the counter, feeling she was being observed, and locked eyes with Vic. She smiled politely and turned her gaze away. Vic felt a surge of butterflies in his stomach, and his nerves carried him away from the boutique.

A short walk later, Vic slung open the door of his small apartment. Now that he was in the privacy of his home, the rage he felt boiled over. He paced back and forth from the living room to the kitchen and back again. Who did this guy think he was, waltzing into town after years away and coming after Shelly? It's not going down like that, he thought. I won't allow it.

He detoured out of the kitchen and into his bedroom. The shades were drawn, cloaking the room in shadows. He approached his bureau, fished a lighter from his pocket and lit two candles, one on each side. The candlelight revealed a mural of photos of Shelly plastered on the wall. He had painstakingly positioned each one to create the perfect balance. He stared at the wall, her beautiful faces looking back at him. Some of them were from years ago, others only days. All of them said the same thing.

He could see it in her eyes in every single photo. She was pleading for him to save her. She needed Vic, and only Vic.

"I know what to do, Shelly," he said to the collage on the wall. "I'll take care of this."

Vic followed the couple from one location to the next over the course of two hours. They met first at the diner. Vic parked a block down the street and waited while they ate. They surprised him by taking a walk around town after dinner, making straight towards his parked truck. He slid down low and leaned across the bench seat. The passenger window was cracked, and he could hear soft conversation and Shelly's musical laughter mixed with the crunch of boots on snow as they passed.

For a moment, he thought he would end it right there. He could slide out of the truck, heavy tire iron in hand, sneak up behind them and bash Aaron's brains out all over the sidewalk. He leaned up and checked the side mirror. Aaron had his arm around Shelly's waist, and she snuggled up tightly against his side. Vic grabbed the door handle with one hand and the tire iron in the other, running on pure rage and adrenaline. He started to pull the handle, but stopped when the jingle of bells from the diner's door rang out and Dotty stepped outside. Vic watched impatiently as she fumbled through her purse. After what felt like an eternity, she pulled her keys from the bag and climbed into her car.

Vic checked the rearview mirror as she pulled away just in time to see Aaron and Shelly turn the corner onto Bradbury Street. He let out a frustrated groan and rapped the tire iron against the dashboard. He started the truck's engine and made a U-turn, following the couple from a safe distance.

He tailed them as they made stops at Croucher's ice cream parlor and Whitman's General Store. By this point, Vic's fiery anger had cooled into a plotting determination, and he was comfortable to wait patiently for the perfect opportunity. He couldn't afford to make a mistake. Shelly was counting on him.

The opportunity he was looking for arrived when Aaron and Shelly pulled off the road by Niederman's pond. Vic watched Aaron pull a couple pairs of ice skates from the trunk of his car, then lead Shelly by hand down to the edge of the frozen water. They strapped on the skates, playfully wobbled their way onto the ice, and then they were off. Aaron took slow and tentative steps, but Shelly accelerated gracefully across the pond. She spun and twirled naturally. For a moment, Vic forgot all about Aaron, enraptured by the beauty of Shelly skating across the ice under the moonlight. The spell was broken when Aaron fell, drawing a chuckle from Shelly. She skated back to the edge of the pond to help Aaron to his feet.

Vic had seen enough. He hopped out of the truck, slid the tire iron into the back of his jeans, fluffed out the back of his jacket to conceal the weapon, and jogged across the road toward the pond.

"Shelly!" he shouted as he slid down the snow-covered embankment.

Shelly and Aaron both turned toward him in surprise.

"Is that Vic?" asked Aaron. A flash of annoyance crossed his face at the interruption.

Vic walked cautiously onto the ice and approached them.

"What's going on here, Vic? Shelly and I are kind of in the middle of something."

Vic looked from Aaron to Shelly. Shelly stared at Vic with contempt.

"Took you long enough," she said.

"I'm sorry," Vic replied.

"I'm confused," Aaron said. "What exactly are you doing out here?"

Vic pulled the tire iron from his pocket in one smooth motion and sent the angled socket end crashing into the back of Aaron's skull. It happened so fast Aaron didn't even raise an arm in defense. The blow dropped him to one knee and then he tumbled over onto his side. He groaned and reached for the back of his head. Blood ran freely onto the ice and a noticeable chunk of his skull had caved in.

Vic pulled back to swing again and finish the job, but Shelly reached out and put a hand on his shoulder, halting him.

"No," she said.

Vic turned to face her. Gone were her soft features and pleasant demeanor. Her eyes glittered with a mad intensity.

"That's too quick."

Vic lowered the tire iron and stepped away from Aaron.

"Break it," she hissed.

Obediently, Vic walked a few steps away and slammed the iron into the ice. The force of the blow caused spiderweb fissures to appear. He drove the iron into the ice again, careful not to stand too close to the now fragile surface. A third and final blow caused a three feet wide section of ice to collapse, revealing a surging darkness beneath. Vic did not need further instruction. He knew what she wanted.

He dropped the tire iron and grabbed Aaron by the shoulders. Aaron tried to object, but his brain was no longer coordinating with his body properly, evidenced by the gore oozing through his bludgeoned and lacerated skull. Vic dragged Aaron to the hole and dropped him into the icy water feet first. Aaron disappeared into the darkness, and for a moment Vic thought he would not surface at all. Then, a hand appeared on the ice below him, followed by a face. Vic and Shelly watched as he slapped weakly at the ice. Vic felt himself deflate as the jealousy and rage fueling him throughout the day vanished, replaced by disgust at what he had done. Shelly laughed softly beside him. It was unpleasant and sharp.

Aaron struggled briefly, but his mental capacities were failing him before the icy water had taken him. The combination of shocks was too much to resist. His lungs filled with water and he sank from view into the darkness below the ice.

"How many more times do I have to do this?"

Shelly wrapped her arms around him from behind. One hand clamped his throat, nails digging into the soft flesh, the other hand squeezing his crotch. She bit down on his earlobe and he groaned in a combination of pleasure, pain, and disgust. "Does it matter? If you want me, then you'll do as I say. You'll take as many as I say. Do you want me, Vic?"

Vic cried out as she tightened both grips.

"DO YOU WANT ME?"

"I do," he sobbed. "I do."

Shelly let go, and Vic dropped to the ice. He turned over onto his side and watched Shelly skate to the edge of the pond and remove the skates. She turned back to him and winked.

"Merry Christmas, lover."

Vic watched her walk away, like he had done so many times before. Already, the guilt of what he'd done was fading. He'd done it out of love. That was all. As she drifted from view, his mind cleared and he smiled, satisfied.

That's what you get, Aaron. That's what you get for messing with my girl. That's what all of you get because she's mine. She's always been mine.

EASTER MORNING

"Good turn out today," said Pastor Jake Rogers. He stood on the sloping front lawn of the church, watching cars pull away. He smiled warmly and waved at each as they passed. A few stragglers were still making their way to the parking lot, dragging children behind them with overflowing Easter baskets.

"Even better than last year," Thomas agreed. He wiped a hand across his brow against a glint of sweat. He was a large man, and despite the crisp spring air, he looked flushed and uncomfortable. "Question is, how do we get them to come back when it's not Easter?"

"Ah, not to worry, Thomas. It's not our place to persuade them. We must be grateful for everyone who comes through our doors, whether it's Easter morning or a Sunday in July. Our job is to give them a place of worship and support when they are ready to receive it."

Thomas nodded. "I know, Jake." He glanced at the driveway curving up the hill from the street to the parking lot. "Not to sound ungrateful for the folks we have, but it sure would be a lot easier to keep this place up if we had more regulars. The drive needs to be repaved, and the fellowship hall roof is just about shot. That takes money, Jake, money we don't have."

Jake smiled and put a reassuring hand on Thomas' shoulder. "The lord will provide. He always does." He gave the shoulder a playful squeeze. "I don't need to make a Doubting Thomas joke, do I?"

Thomas chuckled. "It wouldn't be the first time, would it?"

"I suppose not," Jake replied. "It is hard to resist."

The sound of footsteps crunching on the gravel caused him to turn and look back. A handsome young man smiled and fell in beside them. He was tall and muscular, with neatly combed blonde hair and bright blue eyes.

"What do you think, Jeremy?" asked Pastor Jake.

"Excellent service, sir. I think you really reached some people today."

"Thank you," Jake replied. "I hear from Mrs. Avery that you did a splendid job with the youth group this morning as well."

Jeremy blushed. "They are a great group of kids. I'm honored to teach them."

"They're lucky to have you," Jake said. "If you don't mind, would you care to make a pass through the lawn and make sure all the eggs were collected?"

"Of course," Jeremy said.

The two men watched Jeremy walk swiftly down the hill and around the corner of the church, scanning the lawn for Easter eggs.

"He's a good boy," Thomas said. "The kids love him like crazy." He leaned towards Jake and whispered, "I do believe the young ladies love him like crazy as well."

Jake smiled. "He is an impressive young man. It's rare these days to find a young person so devoted to the church. He's looking into attending a bible college. Says he wants to be a pastor one day."

"Is that a fact? Doesn't surprise me," Thomas replied. He checked his watch and grunted. "I've got to get moving. Cindy's parents are coming over for dinner. I've got to get the grill fired up. Do you need any help before I go?"

"No, sir," Jake replied. "You've been a great help, as always. Enjoy your dinner and tell Cindy's folks I said hello."

"Will do. I'll see you Wednesday evening."

The two shook hands, and Thomas strolled off towards the parking lot. Jake took a deep breath and stared at the clear blue sky. The sun was high and doing an admirable job of knocking the chill out of the air. *The Lord has blessed us this day.* He turned and made his way back to the large wooden doors of the church and stepped inside, thoughts now turned to getting organized for the evening service. He did not hear the muffled cry of pain from around the side of the old building.

Jeremy Higdon stepped swiftly through the yard, scanning the grass for any blips of bright color that didn't naturally belong. He doubted he would find any stray eggs. The children had scoured the yard thoroughly, eager to find any of the prize eggs with five-dollar bills folded neatly inside. He did not mind the task, however. He never felt more at home than he did on the grounds of the church. Any reason to stay here a little longer and delay the gloomy trip home was a welcome respite.

His home life was one of turmoil and upheaval. His parents were at each other's throats or ignoring each other all the time. For the life of him, he could not understand why they stayed together. Financial security was important, but was it worth being miserable? Jeremy supposed in the past they must have been fond of one another, but those days were long gone. When he expressed an interest in going to church, both his parents had supported it, even though neither of them attended. His father was kind enough to drop him off and pick him up in the early days before he got his license. Jeremy figured that every minute he was out of the house at a service or chaperoning a youth group event was a minute they didn't have to feign civility in front of him.

Jeremy had found purpose and direction under the guidance of Pastor Jake. He thought of Jake as more of a father figure to him than his actual father had ever been. Pastor Jake helped people, and that was all Jeremy wanted to do, especially children. If he could provide hope to kids like him who were lost and confused, it would be a life full of purpose and joy.

Jeremy trailed the edge of the property where it butted up against the cemetery. As he expected, it looked like the children had done a fine job of discovering all the eggs. Just as he turned back to the church, he glimpsed someone crouched by a tombstone. From this angle, he could only see the side profile of the man. He was old, with thinning wisps of white hair. He wore a black suit and shiny black dress shoes. The old man was on one knee, both hands gripping the top of the stone, his face to the ground.

Jeremy paused and watched the man for a moment. The safe assumption was he was paying respects to a lost loved one. However, something in the way the man crouched there, head down, called to Jeremy. Perhaps he needed council? Some kind words and an offer of prayer could make a difference. A few times in Jeremy's life, he had felt compelled to intervene. He believed this was God guiding his servant. Now, as he stared at the old man in the cemetery, he felt this way again. Feeling full of spirit, he walked purposefully into the cemetery toward the gravestone.

"Good morning, sir," Jeremy said as he approached. He stopped two rows of gravestones short of the man, not wanting to invade his space unexpectedly. "If you'll allow me, I will offer you words of comfort for your loss. Our doors are always open should you wish to seek fellowship."

"What comfort have you found in those walls, young man?"

"I have found the grace of God."

"Do you believe that to be true?"

Jeremy felt a tinge of discomfort settle over him. "Of course, I do. I feel God's love every day."

"Then why, child, do you find it necessary to hide in those walls instead of being with your family?"

Jeremy felt his heart skip a beat, and his mouth went dry. Before he could reply, the old man spoke again in his gravelly voice.

"If God loves you, then why did he give you parents who care nothing for you? Where is God when you are curled up in bed listening to your parents scream at each other? My young friend, it would seem to me that God has done you a great disservice."

The old man raised his head, showing his face to Jeremy for the first time. Through deep wrinkles, he smiled grotesquely, exposing crooked yellow teeth. His eyes were a sickly green with dark, red-rimmed sacks underneath.

Jeremy stared at the man, horrified. He desperately wanted to turn and run for the church, but his feet seemed pinned to the ground.

"What love is there to be had from a God who tortures his followers? I trust you watch the news from time to time. Such depravity. Sickness, hunger, violence, death, and worse."

"Dear God, give me strength in the face of evil," Jeremy whispered.

"Your prayers fall on deaf ears, my child," the old man hissed. "And you have not seen evil, not yet."

He took a step forward. "I can show you the truth, child."

Another step. "You need not waste your days hiding behind the mask of a faithful servant to a master who cares not for your suffering."

Jeremy watched the man's approach with a detached sense of being. His eyes had glazed over, his mouth agape, a line of drool developing along the bottom lip. His heart hammered in his chest, his body sending up every signal it could to trigger a flight response, but Jeremy had somehow drifted. It now felt as if these things were happening to someone far away.

The man took two more steps, and the distance was closed between them. Had Jeremy been of sound mind, he would have noticed the unnaturally long stride the old man possessed. He grabbed Jeremy by the shoulders with gnarled, age-spotted hands. "Let me show you the truth, Jeremy."

Jeremy gave no signs of acknowledgement, only stared back at the man's cruel face. He did not resist as the old man placed the tip of each pointer finger on Jeremy's temples and pressed firmly.

"See."

Jeremy's eyes rolled back, and he screamed.

Thomas Berry plopped down into the driver's seat of the Chevy Malibu, the frame sinking noticeably under his weight. As he pulled the seatbelt across his barrel chest, he saw Pastor Jake enter the church. He looked nervously around both sides of the car. Satisfied that no one was around, he pulled his phone from the inner breast pocket of his suit jacket.

He lied to Pastor Jake. Carol wasn't expecting him home for another couple of hours. As far as she knew, he was helping Jake put together an itinerary for the following weekend's craft show. He had no concern that she might ask questions to compromise his story. Carol trusted Thomas completely. In their twenty-two years of marriage, she never once had reason to doubt him. They lived comfortably in a nice suburban home. They had no children, a decision they agreed upon. Carol was an elementary school teacher, and she viewed her time with children during the day as enough for her. Thomas was a human resources manager at a manufacturing facility. So far as she knew, it was common for him to have to stay late into the evening hours to work with second shift employees. For many years, there was truth to that. However, his job in human resources would ultimately lead to the temptation that now ruled his life.

A year prior, Thomas interviewed a young woman named Katie for a job opening. She arrived for the interview dressed in a short skirt and a skin tight top with a deep V cut in the front. She wore a half sweater that did little to conceal her breasts pressing out of her blouse. She caught him ogling her as she signed in, and he felt himself blush furiously. He led her to the conference room and closed the door behind them, as per usual.

Throughout the interview, he gathered she was a victim of difficult circumstances. He was limited as to what questions he could ask regarding her past, but she volunteered the information. She was trying to rebuild a life wrecked by poor choices made in desperation. She had spent time in prison on several theft and fraud charges, resulting in losing custody of her child. Finding employment was difficult, her background check stopping potential employers from moving forward. She needed a job, something stable, to put her life back together, and she was running out of options.

Thomas listened to her story with genuine sympathy. He was soft at heart, and he enjoyed helping people better themselves. Unfortunately, he knew that management did not look kindly on past felonies involving theft or violence, making her case a long shot. As he explained how unlikely it was that she would be able to hire on, her demeanor changed. She leaned back in the chair, pushing her chest forward, and relaxed her crossed leg.

"I really need this job," she had said, noting his eyes drawn to her lap. "I'll do anything."

Thomas met her gaze for a moment. Over his years in HR, he had gotten very good at reading people. He could see how disgusted she was with herself for what she was offering, but he also saw that she was determined to see it through.

His heart told him to tell her that wouldn't be necessary. He could push her application through the chain, put in a good word, and fight to get her a chance to prove herself. There would be no need for favors. He would do it because he was a good person and wanted to help her.

That was almost what he did, too.

Instead, he locked the door and took her on the conference room table.

Two weeks later, Katie had an entry-level job on the packaging line, and Thomas had a new obsession. He felt awful for what he had done. Many times, he found himself at his desk, eyes burning with tears as he battled with the guilt of his betrayal. If it ever came out, he would lose everything. His wife, his family, his career, all gone in an instant. Every day, he lived in fear. Through every dinner with his family, every board meeting at work, every church service with the knowing eyes of the crucified Jesus staring into him from the wall behind Pastor Jake's podium, he waited for the shoe to drop. Despite that fear, another feeling was even stronger.

Lust.

He wanted more. Despite everything that could go wrong, he continued to take advantage of Katie's situation. When he had initially suggested to her a *brief meeting* in his office, she had flinched as if he'd struck her. She looked at him with tears brimming and an awful acceptance that this was how it was going to be. A few hours later, she stopped by his office, and he had her again.

So began the cycle that ruled over his life.

Now, with a couple hours to spare before Carol expected him home, he scrolled through the contacts on his phone, stopping on one labeled K. Connelly. He typed out a text message stating he urgently needed to meet and go over a few documents, fat fingers dancing over the screen, and a noticeable bulge developing in his pants. Just as he prepared to hit send, a hand slapped loudly against the car window.

Thomas flailed in the seat, his phone flying from his hands and down onto the floorboard. He turned frantically to the window to see Jeremy standing by the car, his palm pressed flat against the window. He smiled eerily through the glass, filling Thomas with a sense of unease. He reached a quivering hand to the door panel and pressed the button to roll down the window.

"Good Lord, Jeremy. You scared the daylights out of me."

"Why is that, brother Thomas? Were you doing something you shouldn't have?" Jeremy smiled wider.

Thomas blanched. "Of course not. You just startled me. I was just texting Carol that I was on my way home."

"Tsk, tsk," laughed Jeremy. "It's a sin to tell lies. You know that, don't you?" Suddenly, Jeremy stopped smiling. His soft features hardened, and he stared at Thomas with a menacing glare.

Thomas stared back uncomfortably before turning his eyes to his lap. He found he couldn't stand to look at the boy. "Jeremy, I don't understand."

"Oh," Jeremy hissed, "I think you do. I think you understand perfectly. You were going to stop by the shop for a little overtime before you went home, weren't you, Thomas? Miss Connelly needs to pay her union dues, am I right?"

Thomas reeled, looking up at Jeremy with a mixture of shock and horror in his eyes. He started to reply, but the words were trapped in his throat.

"No need to deny it. I know a lot of things. I know a lot of things that you don't know, too." Jeremy said softly, leaning down towards the open window. "Did you know that Katie tried to kill herself after you decided that once wasn't enough? She had the barrel of a pistol in her mouth. She was that close."

Thomas sat silently; eyes fixed in dazed terror on Jeremy.

"But then, and this is the good part, she went another route. She made a mistake, sure, but you took it too far. Do you know what she did, Thomas?"

Thomas shook his head, unaware that tears were now sliding down his cheeks.

"She found out where you lived, and then she paid Carol a visit."

"What?" Thomas choked out.

"That's right," Jeremy said, smirking. "She walked right up to the front door and knocked. Carol, sweet lady that she is, let her right in. She told Carol everything, and I mean *everything*."

"No, I don't believe you."

"Carol was so upset. She waited for you to get home to tell you she was leaving. But the more she thought about it, the more she wanted to pay you back. Leaving you wasn't enough. No, sir. She wanted revenge. She's been getting it too, over and over again. You want to know how?"

Thomas shook his head and sobbed. "Please stop."

Jeremy leaned his head inside the window and whispered, "Carol's been fucking every young stud she can get her hands on."

Thomas cried out in anguish and pushed Jeremy away. Jeremy grabbed him by the wrist and yanked him into the door, his head bouncing off the frame. Pain erupted, and his vision blurred. He felt heat running down the side of his head.

Jeremy grabbed Thomas by the head with both hands and pulled him forward again so his face was clear of the car door.

"It's not enough for you to know, Thomas. You need to see." He pressed a fingertip onto each temple and Thomas howled.

In a flash, Jeremy and the church parking lot disappeared. He found himself looking into his own bedroom. Carol was on the bed, her bare back to him, straddling a muscular young man he didn't recognize. She moaned in ecstasy as she rocked back and forth, increasing the intensity. The 8x10 picture frame of their wedding photo shook and toppled over as a particularly vigorous thrust knocked the headboard into the side table.

Unable to bear witness any longer, Thomas turned away. Standing in the hall behind him was Jeremy. His eyes glowed red, and he snarled. No sign of the kind young man remained.

"You're not Jeremy."

Jeremy gave Thomas a mocking sneer. "I am Jeremy, the way he wants to be now that he has seen the truth. We are together now, and we have no further use for you."

Before Thomas could reply, Jeremy rushed at him with unnatural speed. His hands locked around Thomas's throat. Thomas gasped and clawed at Jeremy's hands, but it was useless. As his vision faded, he caught one more glimpse of Carol bucking wildly on their bed. Then his world faded to black.

Pastor Jake Rogers walked down the narrow hallway off the church chamber to his office. His heart was light. He felt full of spirit this morning, perhaps more so than he had in a very long time. He always tried to keep his sermons upbeat and filled with messages of love and hope for the future. Throughout his life, he had seen many sermons delivered with a message of the terrible fate that awaits those who do not accept Jesus into their lives. Stories of fire and brimstone were great for scaring people, but did little in the way of comfort. Jake wanted his congregation to come to church because it made them feel good, not because they were afraid of what would happen if they didn't. This morning, Jake felt an energy in his words that resonated with every person in attendance. God was working through him, of that, he was sure.

Feeling content, he sat down in the leather chair behind his desk and opened a notebook. He jotted down some talking points for Wednesday evening's service. The Wednesday crowd was always a little smaller, but they tended to be the more receptive of his congregation. He liked to challenge them with deeper discussions to develop them further as students of God's word. He had just begun to lose himself in thought as he outlined his sermon when the heavy wooden door of the church creaked open.

It must be Jeremy, he thought to himself, then continued writing. Jeremy was the most promising of his pupils. He had ascended beyond being satisfied with just accepting God's love. He wanted to spread that love and teach. Jake knew that Jeremy's home life was not ideal, and he welcomed the opportunity to provide some stability for the boy.

"Jeremy," he called out. "I'm in the office."

He waited a few moments, continuing to make notes, but Jeremy did not come.

"Jeremy, is that you?"

Silence.

Frowning, Jake got to his feet and walked out of the office and down the hall. When he emerged into the chamber, he froze. Sitting atop the shoulders of the statue of Jesus on the cross was Jeremy.

"Rejoice, for He has risen!"

Jake stared at Jeremy in blatant confusion.

"For a man of so much talk, you have nothing to say?"

"What are you doing, Jeremy? What is this?"

Jeremy patted the head of the Jesus statue and slid down to the ground, landing in a crouch. "I've been shown the truth," he said. "I see through the lies and fairy tales you've been shoveling me."

Jake watched the boy approach. In an instant of clarity, he understood.

"I'm not talking to Jeremy, am I?"

Jeremy laughed, a grating sound nothing like his usual voice. "I am reborn, Jake. Forgive me for not calling you Pastor, but I no longer follow blindly. The world has become quite clear."

Rather than fear, Jake felt a surge of resolve. This was gratification that he had in fact delivered God's message so purely that the Devil had seen fit to interfere.

"It was very bold of you to enter this place, demon," he said calmly. "Very bold, but very foolish. You are no match for the power of God, and His power is everywhere here. You seek to corrupt a youth in His service, and I will not stand for it."

Jeremy laughed again, closing the distance between them. "What can you do when fear shakes your heart, and you know you will fail? Your faith is weak."

Jake laughed. He leaned over and picked up a bible from the pew to his left. "You are mistaken." He held the book up in front of him and stepped forward. "By the power of God, I demand you leave this child and return to the depths from which you came!"

Jeremy charged at him, covering the remaining few feet between them, and knocked the bible from his hands. They collided and crashed to the ground. Jeremy landed on top and quickly pushed himself up to a mounted position. He threw fists and clawed at Jake's face, snarling in anger.

Jake snatched the boy's wrist, twisted, and rolled him over, pinning him to the ground. "Leave this boy! Disgrace this house of God no longer. I command you by the power of God! I cast you out!"

Jeremy hissed and growled a string of words in a language unknown to man.

For the first time, Jake saw a glimmer of fear in the possessed eyes of Jeremy. The confidence he exuded only moments before was dissipating. This fueled Jake, and he felt the power of God radiating through him.

"You will not have him," he screamed. "I cast you out in the name of Jesus Christ, the son of God!"

Jeremy screamed, writhing in agony. Jake held onto wrists and shouted prayers. Jeremy's struggles increased in intensity, and Jake saw genuine fear in the boy's eyes. For a split second, there was a flash of normalcy on Jeremy's face, and he looked up longingly at Jake, silently begging for help.

Jake renewed his attack with increased urgency. The battle was almost won. The lord was with him.

Sheriff Andrew Young drove down Aukerman Avenue, thinking about how he would spend the rest of the afternoon, when the old man stumbled into the road in front of him. He slammed the brake pedal to the floor, the back end of the cruiser fishtailing to the right, narrowly missing the pedestrian.

"Jesus Christ!"

The old man waved frantically at him, and he rolled down the window.

"Are you okay, sir? You came out of nowhere."

"Murder!" said the old man, gasping for breath.

"Murder?"

"Up at the church. Saw it myself. He killed that man in cold blood!"

Andrew frowned. Between the outlandish claims and the uncoordinated steps of the old man, he suspected the old man was under the influence.

"Sir, have you been drinking?" he asked as he opened the door of the cruiser and climbed out. Before he could maneuver around the open door, the old man slapped his hands on the top of the window frame and was face to face with the sheriff. They locked eyes, and Andrew was no longer convinced the man was drunk. For starters, his breath was atrocious as he panted noxious waves in Andrew's face past dingy yellowed teeth, but there was no trace of the smell of alcohol. The man's eyes were wild with fear. For a moment, Andrew lost himself in the gaze of the old man, the strange flecks of red seeming to beckon him. Then the old man spoke again, bringing him back to attention.

"I was visiting my dear departed wife in the cemetery when I saw it. He killed that man, I tell you. You'd better get up there, Sheriff. I think he might try to hurt the boy."

Andrew gave the man a long, pondering look, then dropped back into the seat of the cruiser.

"You stay here."

The old man nodded and stepped away from the cruiser toward the sidewalk.

Andrew threw the car into drive and drove the half block to the winding driveway up to the church. He took the corner sharply, wheels screeching in protest, and rocketed up the hill. He snatched the radio from the console of the cruiser and pressed the button.

"Tina, stand by. We may have a situation at the Baptist church on Aukerman."

"Did the egg hunt get out of hand?" Tina asked, chuckling.

"I'm not sure what the hell is going on, but stand by. I mean it, Tina."

There was a pause as the dispatcher considered his words.

"Roger that, Andrew. Standing by," she replied, all traces of humor removed from her voice.

Andrew put the radio back and scanned the lawn of the church. As he crested the top of the hill, the parking lot came into view. There were only two cars in the lot, both of which were familiar, and he immediately identified Thomas Berry sitting in his. He pulled the cruiser up beside the gray Malibu and gasped audibly.

Thomas was slumped to the side against the door, his head hanging out the open window. His eyes were wide and bulging, and his mouth hung open. Violent red marks covered his throat, and Andrew didn't need to investigate any further to know they were handprints. Thomas Berry was dead.

His hands shaking, Andrew grabbed the radio again.

"I need backup, Tina, right now." His mind scrambled for the police code, but this sort of thing didn't happen in his town. Not ever. "There's been a murder."

"A murder?" Tina shouted back. "Andrew, what are you-"

"Get me backup, right now God Dammit!"

Andrew threw the radio down into the passenger seat and jumped out of the cruiser. The old man had told the truth about the murder, so he now had no reason to doubt that someone else could be in trouble. *I think he might try to hurt the boy.*

Andrew pulled his service pistol from the holster on his hip and approached the church. As he reached the door, he heard a muffled shout. Gritting his teeth, he pulled the heavy door open and shuffled into the large foyer, gun raised. What he saw stopped him in his tracks.

Pastor Jake was on top of a boy he recognized as Larry Higdon's son. The boy squirmed and tried to free himself from the pastor's grip, but his wrists were pinned. Andrew watched in shock as the pastor screamed in the boy's face.

"Come out, demon!" The pastor's face was blood red, and spittle flew from his mouth with each word.

Andrew fought to overcome the lunacy of what he was seeing. Pastor Rogers was a model citizen. Andrew wasn't a churchgoer himself, but he'd heard nothing but good things about the man. At last, his police instincts took over, and he found his voice.

"Stop!"

The pastor reared back, a thick bible in his hand, eyes wild.

When the state authorities interviewed him later, his statement was he thought the pastor was going to slam the book into the boy's face. He would spend countless nights after asking himself if he had done the right thing. In the heat of the moment, he'd done what he thought he had to do.

He pulled the trigger.

Not once in Andrew's years of service had he ever fired his gun on duty. He did, however, spend a lot of hours on the shooting range, and he did not miss.

The bullet hit home, smashing into the pastor's chest. He spun sideways and slumped to the floor. The boy, sobbing, slid out from under the pastor's legs and raced to Andrew. He wrapped his arms around the cop's waist and wailed.

"He tried to kill me," the boy cried. "He wanted to kill me."

Andrew, numbed by what had just transpired, held the boy silently. His eyes were glued to the body of the pastor, slumped on the floor. He had not moved, and Andrew knew he was dead.

The sound of sirens filled the air.

One after another, police cruisers sped past the old man as he walked down Aukerman Avenue, away from the church. None of the officers so much as glanced at him as they raced by. He smiled, yellow teeth glinting in the sun.

"Rejoice, for He has risen!"

Behind him, church bells sounded the turn of the hour. When the ringing stopped, he was gone.

Acknowledgements

I would like to thank my wife Jessie for always supporting me throughout this process. Writing a book and building relationships with the community takes time away from other things, and she has always been gracious and understanding. I still remember helping wash the dishes after dinner one evening and mentioning I wanted to try writing. She said I should do it, and I haven't looked back. Thanks, babe.

I would also like to thank Matt Wildasin, Chuck Buda, Simon Paul Wilson, JC Walsh, Alex Norcross, Alexander Bailey, and Brandon Applegate for their support. Without Matt's influence and constant support, I don't know that I ever would have started this journey. Chuck lit a fire under me to get this book out there. Sharing his knowledge and experience with me has been invaluable. Simon, JC, Alex, Alexander, and Brandon have been friendly faces in the crowd when I didn't know many people, and I can always count on them for support and guidance. Writing can be a lonely endeavor, and I am grateful to have found friends along the way. You guys are awesome, and this book doesn't happen without you.

Last, but certainly not least, thank you for picking up this book and checking out my work.

About the Author

Steve L Clark is a horror writer from Southwest Ohio where he lives with his wife and three children. Visit steveclarkbooks.com for more info!